Two Much Alike

Bernice Thurman Hunter

Two Much Alike

Cover art by

GINETTE BEAULIEU

Scholastic Canada Ltd.

Scholastic Canada Ltd.
175 Hillmount Rd., Markham, Ontario Canada L6C 1Z7

Scholastic Inc.
555 Broadway, New York NY 10012, USA

Scholastic Australia Pty Limited
PO Box 579, Gosford, NSW 2250, Australia

Scholastic New Zealand Ltd.
Private Bag 94407, Greenmount, Auckland,
New Zealand

Scholastic Publications Ltd.
Villiers House, Clarendon Avenue, Leamington Spa,
Warwickshire CV32 5PR, UK

Canadian Cataloguing in Publication Data

Hunter, Bernice Thurman
Two much alike

ISBN 0-590-24844-8

I. Title.

PS8565.U577T86 2000   jC813'54 C99-932770-4
PZ7.H86Tw 2000

6 5 4 3 2 1   Printed in Canada   0 1 2 3 4 5/0

For Margaret and Mary,
"The Twins."

Contents

Chapter 1

The Taylor Twins

At the supper table Dad loaded up his plate with mashed potatoes, lima beans, savoy cabbage and two porkchops. He always gets two because he's the dad.

After a few satisfying mouthfuls he put his fork down and asked the same dumb question as every other night of the week. "What did you children do in school today?" He always prided himself on taking an interest in his children's schoolwork.

Robbie and Jimmy went right on eating as if they hadn't heard a thing.

"I wrote an essay," Carrie said, chasing a lima bean around her plate. Her teacher calls a story an essay. My teacher calls it a composition. But it's the same thing.

"So did I!" I flattened my mashed potatoes with my knife and drew lines across it with my fork, making it look like a ploughed field. Then I irrigated it with yellow rivers of margarine. "I got an 'A'."

"I got 'A+'," bragged my sister, mushy potatoes squeezing through her teeth.

"Pass the S.P., please," interrupted Robbie from across the table. S.P. is short for salt and pepper. Our mom mixes them together in one shaker. It's handier that way, she says.

Helping herself to the last porkchop, Mom said, "What did you write about, Connie?"

"Well . . ." I tucked a green cabbage leaf underneath my potato field. "Miss Malloy said to write about something important that influences your life, so I wrote about being a twin."

"Did you!" approved Mom.

"And what was your topic, Carrie?" Dad asked as he attacked his second porkchop.

Carrie and I were in different classes. We had been separated in fourth grade because together we had caused too much confusion.

"Mr. Prentice said we could choose our own subject, so I decided to write about Twinship," she said.

"Twinship"! I wished I'd thought of that.

Dad polished off his plate with a heel of bread, then reached for a toothpick from the chicken-shaped eggcup in the middle of the table. "Sounds interesting," Dad said. "How about you girls reading your stories out loud for us?"

Robbie and Jimmy jumped up, nearly knocking over their chairs. "I'm leavin'," Robbie said. "I'm sick of all that twin stuff."

"Me too." Jimmy always agreed with his big brother.

"Then excuse yourself," Mom said.

"They're excused." Dad waved them away. "Okay, let's have it," he said.

Carrie and I went to get our book bags from the hall

bench where we'd dropped them.

"He might be mad at what I wrote," Carrie whispered.

"I'm thinking the same thing," I whispered back.

Mom and Dad were waiting expectantly.

"You first, Connie," Dad said.

I took a deep breath and began:

"Ives Elementary School, June 1, 1953.

"On being a twin, by Constance Taylor.

"My sister and I are identical twins, which means we were hatched from the same egg. We were both born on May the sixteenth, 1942, in Detroit General Hospital. My sister's name is Carrie, short for Caroline. She has no middle name and neither do I. That's because our mom was not expecting two babies because we only weighed as much as one — four pounds each. I think the most interesting thing about us is that we are mirror twins. That means Carrie is left-handed and I am right-handed. But we are both ambidextruss."

Carrie gave a little huff and Dad said, "Shhh. You'll have your turn, Carrie. Go ahead, Connie."

"It's fun being identical because you can fool people most of the time. Even your own parents. Our parents are nice." Here came the part that might make Dad mad, so I lowered my voice. "But our dad is old-fashioned and he still believes in spankings." Then I hurried on.

"We were very cute when we were little. You can tell by our pictures. Mom dressed us exactly alike and parted our hair right down the middle so nobody could tell which was which. When I look at the pictures I can't even tell myself! We have two brothers. Robbie is the oldest, he's fifteen. Carrie and I come next, we are eleven. Our other brother Jimmy is the youngest. He's nine and he's a pest."

Dad and Mom laughed and Carrie huffed again.

"I like being twins because we are best friends and we share everything: clothes and toys and work. We have to help with the dishes every night and clean our room on Saturdays. But it only takes half as long because there are two of us. That's all I can think of to say right now. I hope I get a good mark for this composition. The end."

Dad clapped his hands and Mom said, "Very good, Connie! Now yours, Carrie."

"Mine's practically the same as hers," she said.

"Let's have a look," Dad said. Pushing aside his coffee cup he placed the papers side by side on the table in front of him. Then his eyes darted back and forth from one to the other. "Well, I'll be darned," he said, scratching his head. "They're almost identical. You two must have collaborated."

"No, we didn't!" we protested in one voice.

Dad shook his head and handed the papers to Mom. After reading them both she turned to Carrie with a puzzled frown. "There's just one thing that's different," she said. "Carrie, why on earth did you say that being a twin makes you feel like half a person?"

"Because it does. Nobody ever calls us by name. It's always 'the twins.' Like when Aunt Sylvia asks about us, she never says 'How's Carrie doing?' or 'How's Connie?' It's always, 'How are the twins?'"

"Oh, fiddlesticks," Dad said. Then he turned to me. "By the way, Connie, why did you sign your name Constance?"

"Because Miss Malloy said she wouldn't accept nicknames. I sure wasn't going to use my real name. It's the stupidest name in the world."

"It's no such thing," huffed my mother, dishing up the rice pudding. "Conroy was my grandmother's maiden name and I'm proud of it."

"And Caroline's a beautiful name," Dad said, nodding his head. "It was my mother's name."

"Caroline's nice," Carrie agreed.

"Oh sure," I said. "Lucky for you!"

"Well, how about Rob-bit-son," snorted Robbie. He and Jimmy had come back for dessert.

"That's worst of all!" Carrie and I squealed.

"Jameson is dopey, too," put in Jimmy, not wanting to be left out.

"They're all lovely family names," Mom said.

"And you children should be proud to carry them," Dad added.

"Tell us about the night we were born, Mom." Carrie and I loved that story.

"Oh no, not again," protested Robbie. Scraping their dessert dishes clean in seconds, he and Jimmy disappeared again.

"Aren't you two getting too old for that story?" asked Dad.

"We'll never be too old," we said emphatically.

Mom got a dreamy look in her eyes as she stirred a saccharine tablet into her black coffee. "You were born on my thirtieth birthday, and when they told me I had twin girls I said I could think of better things to get for a birthday present." She rolled her eyes and laughed. Then she added with a squinch of her nose, "I was only kidding, of course. Well, Carrie arrived first, at 2:00 A.M."

"Wrong," Dad butted in. "Connie came first, then Carrie."

"Well, I guess I should know," huffed Mom.

"How? You were out like a light by then," scoffed Dad. "I remember it as if it was yesterday. The first one they showed me was Connie and I noticed right away that her right ear was bent. Then ten minutes later out came Carrie and I saw that her left ear was bent. And when I questioned Dr. Duncan about it she said it was because they were mirror twins. So — end of argument." Dad scraped back his chair and got up.

As he left the kitchen he shot a parting glance over his shoulder at us twins. "By the way," he said, "you both spelled ambidextrous wrong."

Mom was at the sink running water into the dish pan. She added a flurry of Lux Flakes, and soap bubbles full of rainbows sailed up around her head. "The least you twins could do," she said, sounding miffed because she'd lost the argument, "is pick up a dish towel."

Chapter 2

Trading Places

That night Carrie and I traded bunks.

"Carrie." I threw her pillow up and she threw mine down. "Have you ever been sorry we're twins?"

"Sometimes," she said. "I hate it when people ask Mom which is which. That makes me feel like a thing. And I get tired of being called by your name."

Stretching my right leg straight up, I kicked the lump she made in the springs above me. She leaned over the rail and grinned down at me. It was like looking in a mirror. The same oval face and gold-speckled green eyes and light brown hair waving over her shoulders. "I've got an idea," she said. "Let's dye our hair. You be blonde and I'll be brunette."

"Why?"

She crossed her arms over the rail and leaned her chin on her hands. "Just to be different."

"Then you do wish we weren't twins!" I clasped my hands behind my head and glared up at her.

"Oh . . ." she flopped over on her back out of sight.

"I do like all the extra attention we get."

"Yeah. And all the stuff we get away with," I laughed. "Do you want to switch places with me tomorrow? I'll be in Mr. Prentice's class and you be in Miss Malloy's?"

"Okay. What'll we wear?"

That was the only way people could tell us apart. Our Mom always bought us different coloured dresses. Carrie got pink and I got blue. Or, if my dress was yellow, Carrie's would be green. Always the same style. Just different colours. Mom started it when we were little because sometimes she couldn't tell us apart herself.

"Do you remember the first time we switched clothes, Carrie? We were about four and we fooled both Mom and Dad. Then Daddy noticed my bent right ear because I'd tucked my hair behind it."

Carrie laughed and her head popped over the rail again. "You know the first thing I remember?" she said. "I remember the day I stole your bottle right out of your mouth and finished it before Mom came back and she couldn't figure out why you cried all night."

We often traded memories like that. I thought how boring it must be not to have a twin to share special memories with.

"What shall we wear tomorrow?" Carrie asked.

"I haven't worn your red dress yet."

"It's in the wash basket."

"Well . . . how about our corduroy jumpers? You wear my green one and I'll wear your brown one."

"Okay. And our white blouses."

Just then Dad's voice came booming up the stairs. "Do you two want me to come up there?"

"NO!" we chorused.

We settled down then and went to sleep without getting spanked that night.

* * *

The next day we made a fatal mistake. We forgot to switch homework and we both got caught and had to stay in after school and write lines. Miss Malloy made me write "I promise I will not change places with my sister again because it is deceitful." I had to write it fifty times. So she made me tell fifty lies!

Mr. Prentice made Carrie write "Changing places with my twin sister is a form of duplicity!" She had to write it fifty times, too, but she didn't have to use the word "promise" so her lines were not lies. And she said she didn't mind writing all those lines because she learned the meaning of a swell new word: duplicity.

Chapter 3

Passing Reward

On the last day of school we ran all the way home waving our report cards over our heads. We had both got honours, but Carrie got one more mark than I did.

Bursting in the kitchen door we cried, "Where's Mom?"

Jimmy was standing at the counter slathering Planters peanut butter on a piece of bread. "She went shopping down Jefferson Street," he said.

So we ran upstairs and hid our report cards under our mattresses so Jimmy wouldn't find them. (We had caught him red-handed once searching our room. For evidence, he said, but he never would tell us what he was trying to prove.) Changing into our play clothes, we raced outside.

We were right in the middle of a game of hide-and-seek with the neighbourhood kids when Mom came staggering up Newport Street loaded down with shopping bags. Almost dropping them on the sidewalk, she wiped the sweat off her brow and lifted her short black hair with her fingers to let the breeze blow through.

"Connie!" She knew me easily by my play dress. With my forehead pressed to the telephone pole, I was counting by twos to one hundred. "Come here and give me a hand! Where's your sister?"

"She's hiding. Can't we finish our game first?"

"No! Come and help me now!"

Mom must never have played hide-and-seek when she was a kid, I thought, because if she had she'd know that you weren't supposed to stop in the middle of counting to one hundred by twos.

Cupping my hands around my mouth I yelled, "CARR-IE! Ollie-ollie-in-free! We gotta help Mom."

My twin popped up from behind a spirea bush with little white berries clinging to her hair like pearls.

It was our job to put the dry goods away in the pantry while Mom stocked up the Frigidaire.

"Have you seen the boys?" Mom asked, wiping crumbs and peanut-butter smears off the Formica counter.

"Jimmy's probably upstairs snooping," I said, filling the sugar bowl. Then I wet my finger and stuck it in and licked it. "And I saw Robbie go in next door with Betty Pool."

"Yeah. And they were holding hands," snitched Carrie.

"Don't tattle," Mom said, tying on her apron.

When we finished our job we raced upstairs to get our report cards.

Brushing flour off her hands onto her apron, Mom took them and read them carefully, one by one. As she read, her pretty face was wreathed in smiles. Too bad we had to take after our dad, I thought for the hundredth time, then instantly I felt guilty because Dad wasn't too bad looking for a forty-five-year-old person. Funny how the boys looked like our Mom with their dark wavy hair and big blue eyes and we favoured our dad with our sandy hair and brown-speckled green eyes. You'd think it would be the other way around.

"Your dad will be pleased as Punch with these report-cards," Mom said.

The minute Dad stepped in the door, before he even got his shirt-sleeves rolled up, Carrie and I thrust our report cards at him.

He was pleased as Punch, and he was satisfied with the boys' report cards too.

"Can we do something special to celebrate, Dad?" we asked in unison. Our dad always gave us kids a reward for passing. Last year he had taken us to Tiger Stadium to see a baseball game. And the Detroit Tigers had beat the Baltimore Orioles all hollow.

He frowned and stroked his chin as if he had to think about it. Then he said, "Would a trip to Toronto be special enough?"

"YAY!" All four of us kids screamed at the top of our lungs.

We loved going to Toronto because Dad's family lived there and we had dozens and dozens of Canadian cousins. Dad had been born and raised in Toronto but he had moved to Detroit, Michigan, during the Great Depression to get a job at the Ford Motor Company.

Mom had been born in Nottingham, England. She had come all the way over to America by herself in 1934, so we never saw her family. She had landed a job at the Ford Motor Company, too, and that's where she met our dad.

* * *

"We'll take the scenic route," Dad said as he headed north out of Detroit on Highway 94.

The boys were in the back seat of "Boris Karloff" (that's what Robbie had nicknamed our 1948 Ford station wagon) and Carrie and I sat in the middle seat behind Mom and Dad. Dad wouldn't drive anything but a Ford because he said he owed it to old Henry (Henry Ford, that is). "He gave me a job when I couldn't find one for love nor money in Canada," he always says.

The most exciting part of the trip, besides getting there, was always crossing the border. The customs officer put his head inside our car and looked at all us kids. "These all yours?" he asked.

"No. I kidnapped the lot of them and I'm going to sell them in Canada," our dad said with a straight face. "I hear they pay big money up there for strays . . . especially twins."

Rolling her eyes at the uniformed man Mom assured him that she couldn't give us away if she wanted to and Dad showed him his driver's licence. Then the man grinned and winked and waved us on.

As we passed under the big sign that said "Welcome to Canada" a funny, shivery feeling ran up my spine. Being in a foreign country was sort of scary, like going into the wrong classroom by mistake.

Over the skyscraping Blue Water Bridge we glided, while down below, sailboats skimmed along the sparkling green waters of the St. Clair River.

After a couple of travelling hours we kids started to get fidgety. "Are we nearly there?" Carrie and I yelled over the hot wind blowing in the windows.

"No!" Mom was frantically tucking flying tendrils of shiny black hair under her chiffon kerchief, trying to keep it nice.

"Can I come up there and sit on you, Mom?" yelled Jimmy, his face shoved between Carrie and me.

"Shut up and get back in your own seat." I twisted around and pushed his face. "You nearly broke my eardrum."

"You all better start behaving yourselves." Dad was glaring at us in the rear-view mirror. "Or for two cents I'll turn around and head straight back home."

"Read your books and be quiet," Mom advised.

"I chuck up when I read in the car," Jimmy complained.

"Then play I-spy-with-my-little-eye!" Mom's voice was getting hoarse from screaming over the passing trucks.

"The twins won't play with me," whined Jimmy.

"Well, maybe Robbie will." Mom cranked up the window and started fanning herself with a Silver Screen magazine. Bette Davis was on the cover. Mom called her "Bet." "I'd rather be hot than listen to the roar of those lorries," she said. That's what Mom called trucks — lorries — because she was English.

"Robbie's asleep," Jimmy yelled back.

"We're hungry!" Carrie and I put in.

"Oh, for Pete's sake!" bellowed Dad. The tires squealed and we all lurched over to one side as he swung the car off the highway into a truck stop.

When we were all watered and fed, including Boris Karloff, we piled back in and promised to be good the rest of the way.

Our Canadian Cousins

"City of Toronto. Population 650,000!" announced Robbie.

"Are we here?" Jimmy woke up with a start.

"We're here in record time," Dad said proudly.

Half an hour later Mom put her head out the window. "I think we're lost," she said. "I don't recognize this district."

"We're not lost!" Dad exploded. "I know Toronto like the back of my hand."

Mom rolled her eyes. "Well, you'd better stop for petrol," she said. That was gasoline in Mom's English talk. "The little arrow is right on empty."

Dad pulled into a Joy filling station. As soon as the car stopped, Mom hopped out to ask for directions.

* * *

Our first stop was Aunt Minnie and Uncle Emery's house. They lived in Islington, on the outskirts of Toronto.

"What's Emery doing with a Chevy?" Dad said as he

pulled into their driveway and blasted the horn. He thought everybody should drive a Ford.

The screen door flew open and out on the back porch came Aunt Min and Uncle Emery, followed by fat Cedric. Cedric was their only child. He was about our Robbie's age. Mom always said, with a roll of her eyes, that the sun rose and set on Cedric.

Uncle Emery yanked open the car door. "How's my two sweetpeas-in-a-pod?" he hollered. Uncle Emery had got deaf from shelling during the war so he hollered at everybody.

"We're fine!" we hollered back. Then we jumped out of the car and chased each other all over their big back-yard to get the pins and needles out of our feet.

Aunt Minnie had lunch all ready on the kitchen table: salmon sandwiches and French-Canadian pea soup and lime Jell-O. Between bites, Dad harangued Uncle Emery about driving a Chevrolet. Mom and Aunt Minnie ignored them and exchanged family gossip. Mom bragged about all our high marks and Aunt Minnie said Cedric had done even better but she couldn't remember for the life of her where she had put his report card. Mom rolled her eyes.

After lunch the boys went outside to compare cars, and Carrie and I ran upstairs to the bathroom. On the wall at the top of the stairs hung an old-fashioned oval frame with a picture of a boy in uniform. He stared out from under the peak of his army cap with painted-blue eyes.

"He looks a bit like our dad," Carrie whispered. "But I can't remember who he is."

"I think he would have been our uncle," I whispered

back. There was something about his sad blue eyes that made us whisper. "But he got killed in the War."

The eyes followed us as we passed, giving us a creepy feeling, so as soon as we were finished in the bathroom we raced downstairs again. The grownups were still gossiping over their tea so Carrie and I started chasing each other in circles through the living room and dining room and back into the kitchen.

"There's no running in my house!" squeaked Aunt Minnie. She had a high, squeaky voice like a mouse.

"Sit down and behave yourselves," ordered our dad.

"Oh, leave the sweetpeas alone," grinned Uncle Emery. "They're only young once."

Then Mom hopped up and said, "Well, we must be on our way. We've got lots of visiting to do. We'll see you folks later in High Park." Then she whispered aside to us. "When we get to the park you can run to your heart's content."

Chapter 5

Taylor Family Picnic

We didn't come over from Detroit to Toronto very often, because it was hundreds of miles. But whenever we did, we always had a big Taylor family picnic in High Park — the biggest park in Toronto, Dad says.

There were about twenty-five kids in the Taylor family, all ages and shapes and sizes. At first we were a bit shy with one another. But once we started playing a game of tag we soon got over it.

Fat Cedric couldn't run very fast but he managed to grab my hair as I went flying by.

"I tagged you, Connie! You're it!" he shouted.

"I'm not Connie, I'm Carrie," I lied with a grin.

Usually Carrie and I got a big kick out of fooling people. But this time she surprised me. "Stop pretending you're me!" she snapped.

I just gaped at her with my mouth open. Then I decided she must be joking and I burst out laughing.

"How on earth do you tell them apart?" I heard

Auntie Bea ask my mother. "They're as alike as two brown eggs."

Auntie Bea was Uncle George's wife. Uncle George was the youngest of Dad's nine brothers and sisters. Eight not counting the dead soldier. They had two little girls named Anne and Louise who wore matching glasses and looked almost as much alike as Carrie and I did.

"It's not easy," Mom laughed.

"It's easy if you know how," Dad said. "Come over here, you two."

"He's going to make us show our ears," I said.

"Oh, I'm so sick of that ear stuff," grumbled Carrie. "Let's pretend we don't hear him." So we ran the other way.

Just then our cousin Peter said, "Let's go down to the zoo and see the animals."

So the pack of us went skipping down the hill, leaping over flower beds and darting through the trees like antelopes.

Behind a high wire fence were camels and goats and dappled deer. And on the far side of the paddock a huge grey elephant was slurping water from a wooden tub with its wrinkled trunk.

The camels lifted their heads and stared at us. A mother deer with shiny black button eyes ambled over, followed by her babies.

Carrie and I stuck our lips through the wire fence and made kissing sounds to coax the babies closer. The fawns were a matching pair. They had spotted coats and powder-puff tails and black button eyes like their mother's.

"They're identical," I whispered to Carrie. "Just like us."

Peggy, Peter's teenaged sister, who was known in the family as "Pretty Peggy," was standing beside us. "I wouldn't want to be a twin," she said.

"Why not?" I snapped at her.

"Because you have no identity," she said. Tossing her long black mane she galloped off before I had a chance to contradict her. She's not so pretty, I thought. She looks like a big old horse.

"She's just jealous," I said to Carrie.

"Oh, Connie," she said. "Not everybody wants to be a twin, you know."

I could hardly believe my ears. But before I got a chance to answer Dad appeared on top of the hill, his hands cupped around his mouth like a megaphone. "Come and get it!" he hollered.

* * *

Three picnic tables were fitted together to make a long family table. Paper tablecloths fluttered along the benches. The tables groaned with food: huge bowls of potato and macaroni salads, hard-boiled eggs, bologna and salmon sandwiches, pickles, and red radishes the size of golf balls. For dessert there were cakes and tarts and a huge round watermelon bigger than a beach ball. And placed at intervals along the table were five huge bottles of orange soda and three Thermos bottles: two full of tea and one full of coffee.

Carrie made a dash for the empty seat between Peggy and Peter.

"Hey! There's no room for me," I complained.

"Well, sit over there," Carrie said, pointing across the

table to the empty spot between Mom and Jimmy. Wiggling in between them, I got the strangest feeling that Carrie wanted to get rid of me.

"Where're my sandwiches?" demanded our Dad.

"Oh, no!" cried his sister, Janet. "If you mean what I think you do I'm leaving." She got up in a huff and went to the other side of the table.

Sure enough Mom had brought Dad's favorite sandwiches wrapped in waxed paper and double-wrapped in the *Detroit Free Press*: Limburger cheese spread with Keene's mustard between thick slices of Italian bread.

"Why do you let him eat that stuff?" gasped Aunt Lily, pinching her nose. Mom laughed and rolled her eyes.

"Thank goodness we're out in the open air is all I've got to say," cried Uncle Lyle, waving the smell away with his paper plate.

Dad grinned and took a big bite of his smelly sandwich. Jimmy was the only one who would help him eat them.

It was a sumptuous, marvellous, boisterous picnic. By the time the tables were cleared, the sun was slanting eastward through the trees and we kids were ready to drop. Actually Carrie and I did drop, right onto the soft-mown grass. I was nearly asleep, the sun darkening behind my eyelids, when Mom cried, "Up you get, you two. Your dad's running out of patience."

Boris Karloff's horn was honking steadily, so we scrambled to our feet. Robbie and Jimmy were already in the back seat.

Carrie and I both yawned and rubbed our eyes and said, "Where are we going to sleep tonight?"

"Where would you like to?" Mom asked. "We've got several invitations."

She didn't have to ask us twice. All four of us kids hollered, "Auntie Rose and Uncle Dave's house!"

Uncle Dave and Auntie Rose and their two boys had not come to the picnic. They had gone to visit Auntie Rose's mother in the hospital. But Mom had called her on the phone from Aunt Minnie's.

Uncle Dave was our Dad's older brother. Every time he laughed he coughed his head off because he smoked too many cigarettes. We liked Uncle Dave but Auntie Rose was our favorite. She was lots of fun and she let us have the run of the house. Our other aunts were very prim and proper. You had to sit still on their brocade chesterfields and keep your hands out of the jelly-beans in their cut-glass candy dishes.

Canadians call their sofa a chesterfield. Mom said that's because it was invented by an Englishman named Lord Chesterfield. Dad said, "Oh, that's baloney!" But Mom is English so she should know.

Chapter 6

Which Is Which?

Bart and Norman, Uncle Dave and Auntie Rose's sons, were our favourite cousins. Especially Bart, the younger one. Norman was nearly a man. He was nice and we liked him but Bart was the most fun.

After a light supper, Uncle Dave tilted his chair back and fished an orange two-dollar bill out of his pocket. (Canadian money is all different colours, like Monopoly money.) Then he sent all us kids to Bloor Street for two bricks of Neapolitan ice cream. "You're in charge, Norman," he said. "And I'm having an ice cream fit. So hurry there and hurry back." Laughing at his own joke, he had a coughing fit.

I didn't care who was in charge as long as it wasn't Robbie.

The Jersey Ice Cream Parlour had a big picture of a Jersey cow in the window. A bubble coming out of its mouth said, "I make gooood ice-cream!" We got in a long lineup that stretched right out to the street. When we finally reached the counter, a lady in a blue smock looked at Carrie and me and did a double-take. "Oh, twins!" she squealed. "Aren't they cute!" Turning to Norman she said, "How do you tell your sisters apart?"

"They're not my sisters," laughed Norman. "They're my American cousins. And I can't tell which is which."

Under her breath I heard Carrie mutter, "Which is which, which is which," in a really sarcastic voice. She'd never done that before. I was glad no-one heard her but me.

* * *

Uncle Dave cut the Neapolitan bricks into squares and Auntie Rose served them up on green glass plates. Each square was neatly divided into three flavours: vanilla, strawberry and chocolate. The three colours made a pretty picture on the green glass plates.

Licking the back of her spoon, Auntie Rose said to Mom, "Do you remember the time I minded the twins and I took their name tags off to bathe them? Then I couldn't tell which was which?"

"I do." Mom smiled and nodded her head. "It was their first visit to Toronto. They were only three months old and without the name tags I couldn't tell them apart myself."

Carrie and I looked at each other suspiciously. "Do you suppose," I said, "that I'm really Caroline and she's really Conroy?" I hoped so because I liked Carrie's name better than mine.

"Of course not." Dad snorted, dashing my hopes. "I've known which was which from day one because of your ears. Now you kids finish your ice cream. It's time you were all in bed."

It was great fun going to bed at Auntie Rose and

Uncle Dave's. Their house was upside-down and stuck on the side of a hill. It was opposite to a normal house because the kitchen and living room were upstairs and the bedrooms were downstairs, with sliding doors opening out into the steep backyard. Carrie and I shared a pull-out couch and the boys slept on mats on the floor.

The next morning Auntie Rose made a great big breakfast of bacon and eggs and pancakes and toast and orange juice and coffee.

Jimmy wolfed a whole plateful down and asked for a second helping.

"You've had enough," Dad said. "I don't want you chucking up on the way home."

"That's right," Uncle Emery said. "It's a long way back to Motown." That's what he called Detroit, Michigan — Motown, which is slang for Motor City.

Chapter 7

Home Again

"Did you have a good time?" Mom asked us. She didn't have to shout because the weather had got cooler and the car windows were all rolled up.

"Yeah, we had lots of fun." I answered for Carrie and me. "When we go back to school in the fall and the teacher asks us to write a composition about what we did on our summer holidays we can write about our trip to Toronto."

"I'm not going to write about it," Carrie said.

"Why not?"

"Because I want my story to be different than yours. Remember what Peggy said about twins having no identity? Well, I want to be different."

"Oh, she's just jealous. I already told you that."

"How do you know if she's jealous? You don't know everything."

"You don't know everything," repeated Jimmy.

"Shut up, I'm trying to read back here," grumbled Robbie.

"Shut up, I'm trying to read back here," mimicked Jimmy.

"Say one more word and I'll brain you," threatened Robbie.

"Say one more word . . . " teased Jimmy.

"Stop that, Jimmy!" Mom cried.

"Stop that, Jimmy!"

All of a sudden Dad slammed on the brakes and we all lurched forward. Twisting around, he glowered at Jimmy. "Are you going to quit that, or am I going to have to . . ."

"Okay, okay!" Jimmy cowered back in his seat. "Gee whiz, a guy can't have any fun."

Merging back into the stream of traffic on Highway 2 Dad said, "Now all of you be quiet or this will be our last trip to Toronto." Then Mom turned around and warned us with a finger to her lips.

Carrie went to sleep with her face plastered on the window.

I stared out the other window at the boring scenery and thought about what Peggy had said. Darn her, I thought, us twins are none of her business.

We dozed most of the way home and it was night by the time we got there. It wasn't until Boris Karloff pulled up in front of our house on Newport Street and we stumbled out of the car that Mom noticed Carrie's face was red. Feeling her forehead anxiously, she said, "She's burning up with fever!"

Dad leapt up the veranda steps and unlocked the door, and Mom helped Carrie into the house and up to bed. Robbie and Jimmy and I went into the kitchen to have a snack. Then we all went to bed without an argument.

Mom was sitting on the edge of the lower bunk sponging Carrie from a basin of water. I climbed up the ladder into my own bunk. It felt nice and cozy after the lumpy pull-out couch at Auntie Rose's house. I fell asleep instantly.

In the morning Carrie was no better. Mom called the doctor and she came right over. She examined Carrie and wrote out a prescription for penicillin. Carrie had scarlet fever.

I expected to get it, too, because we always got sick together. But this time we didn't. Carrie had to be isolated in our room, so I had to sleep on the living room sofa, which was just about as lumpy as Auntie Rose's couch.

* * *

Carrie was very sick, and it took a long time for her to recover. She got skinny and pale, and her hair fell out. When it started growing back, it was curly. My hair was still long and wavy, so when school started in September we weren't identical anymore.

The change gave me a peculiar, panicky feeling that I'd never felt before. On the first day of school, Ruby Butternick called to us from across the street.

"Hey, Carrie! Are you all better now?" Ruby had never been able to tell us apart before. Especially from across the street.

"Hey, Ruby!" Carrie was thrilled to be recognized and was about to run across when I grabbed her arm.

"Just a darn minute," I snapped. "Are you going to leave me standing here alone?"

"You can come if you like."

"No. I want you to walk to school with me like always. Just the two of us."

"Oh, Connie, stop being such a baby. Remember what cousin Peggy said? Well, now's my chance to . . . to . . . to individuate. I don't want to be half a person all my life." Yanking her arm away from me she ran across to join Ruby.

So for the first time in our lives, I walked to school on the first day by myself. This year I was in Miss Markle's sixth grade class. Carrie got Mr. Bradley.

As the weeks went by, Carrie's hair grew longer and the tight curls loosened into soft waves. We were nearly identical again. I was glad, but Carrie wasn't.

"Mom," she said one day when she was peering at herself in the kitchen mirror. "Can I get a permanent wave? I liked my hair when it was curly. And Ruby said it really suited me."

I was just about to protest when Mom saved me the trouble. "You and Connie were both blessed with lovely heads of hair. And your father is so proud of your natural waves. You want to spoil it with a frizzy permanent? The answer is no!"

I felt like cheering, but I didn't.

Chapter 8

No More Spankings

Dad had not spanked us all the time Carrie was sick and while she was convalescing. So one night when we were throwing our pillows up and down and laughing like hyenas, he took us by surprise and came pounding up the stairs.

Twice he had hollered up with a warning, but we hadn't paid any attention, so by this time he was mad as a hornet and spanked us both really hard. Carrie cried, and I almost did.

"It's not fair," she whimpered. I could tell her feelings were hurt more than her backside.

"It's stupid and humiliating, too," I said, lying on my stomach rubbing my behind. "We're too old for spankings. I'll bet none of our friends get spanked."

"Ruby and Roy Butternick have never been hit in their lives," sniffled Carrie. "Ruby says her parents don't believe in corporal punishment."

"What's corporal mean?" I didn't like it when she used a word I didn't know.

"Umm . . . it means punishment that hurts . . . something like that."

Ruby and Roy were the only other set of twins in our school. Of course, they weren't identical because one was a girl and one was a boy. But they looked alike, just the same, with carroty red hair and green eyes and freckles.

"Well, what can we do about it?" I wondered.

"Maybe we could ask Mom to speak to Dad," Carrie suggested.

We were quiet for a minute, thinking, then we both said at once, "No. Let's talk to him ourselves."

"When?" asked Carrie.

I leaned over the rail again and looked into my identical face. "Tomorrow," I said.

"DO YOU WANT ME TO COME BACK UP THERE?" Dad bellowed from down below.

"NO!" we bellowed back.

We shut up then and went to sleep.

* * *

The next night after supper when Dad was relaxing in his La-Z-Boy reading the *Detroit Free Press*, Carrie and I went in and stood on either side of his chair.

We took a deep breath and said, "Dad."

He looked up with a grin. He always got a kick out of our synchronized talking. But when he saw the serious look on our faces his grin turned to a frown.

"What's the matter?" he asked.

"Nothing," we said, "But . . ."

"But what?"

"Well . . . we want to talk to you about something serious."

Lowering the newspaper, he looked at us over his

32

reading glasses. "Spit it out," he said.

So we blurted the words out together. "We're eleven years old and we don't think we should be spanked anymore."

"Give me two good reasons," he said.

"It's humiliating," Carrie said.

"And old-fashioned," I said.

"And nobody gets spanked anymore," we said together.

"Well, my father used his belt on me until I was fifteen and it didn't do me a lick of harm," Dad said stubbornly.

Mom looked up from the armchair where she was darning socks. "Times have changed since we were young, and corporal punishment has gone the way of corsets. Why, I've heard that in England it's against the law to spank your children."

Dad folded his newspaper. He took off his glasses and cleaned them with his handkerchief. Then he stood up and crossed his arms and looked down at us. When he spoke, his voice was dead serious. "I work hard all day long making motor-cars on a noisy assembly line," he said, "and when I come home at night I think I deserve some peace and quiet, don't you?"

"Yes," we said, nodding our heads.

"Well . . . do you think you two could stop fooling around at night and behave like normal human beings?"

Carrie and me looked at each other. Then we looked at our dad. "We could try," we said.

Covering his mouth with his hand, as if he was hiding a smile, he said, "Then go to bed and try."

Dad plunked back into his chair and cracked open his newspaper, holding it up in front of his face. "The

English," he muttered, "what do they know."

Mom rolled her eyes and went into the kitchen. We followed her to kiss her good night. "I'm proud of you!" she whispered. Then we ran upstairs and threw Jimmy out of the bathroom.

We got undressed without saying a word and climbed into our bunks. About five minutes went by before I dared lean over the bar. Carrie was staring up at me, her speckled eyes twinkling.

"Do you think we can do it?" I whispered.

"No." Her whisper came out on a snicker.

Flopping over on our stomachs we buried our faces in our pillows and smothered ourselves to sleep.

We tried hard to behave after that. And we managed not to get spanked anymore. But we came close a couple of times.

Chapter 9

Absolutely Identical

It was nearly the end of October before I realized that we still were not absolutely identical.

"Hi, Connie!" Ruby Butternick was behind me in line. If Ruby could tell us apart from the back, then there must be something wrong. So I dragged Carrie into the school nurse's office.

Miss Christmas looked up and smiled. She wore a white coat and white cap with a black band around it. The black band proved she was a real nurse. "Hello, Bobbseys," she said. She always jokingly called us the Bobbsey Twins. "What can I do you for?" That was her other joke.

"We need to get weighed," I said.

"Mom didn't tell us to," Carrie objected.

"Yes, she did. You just didn't hear because you were arguing with Robbie."

She believed me because we were always arguing with our brothers about something.

Miss Christmas measured and weighed me first. I was

five feet tall and weighed eighty-seven pounds. Then she measured Carrie. "Four feet, eleven and a half inches," she said. "Now hop up on the scale." She moved the bob back and forth across the bar until it was perfectly balanced. "Hmm," she pursed her lips. "The last time I took your vital statistics they were exactly the same."

Sitting down at her desk she wrote a note on an Rx pad and sent it home with Carrie in a sealed envelope. Mom looked worried when she read it. But she put it on the windowsill and didn't say anything.

When Dad came home she showed him the note before supper. Usually she didn't confront him with family problems until after he'd eaten. Mom's motto was: Feed him first, then tell the worst.

It must be serious if it couldn't wait, I thought.

He read the note, then he put a finger under each of our chins and tipped our heads back. After a close scrutiny he said to Mom, "Carrie's face is thinner than Connie's."

"I'll call Dr. Mary and make an appointment first thing tomorrow morning," Mom said.

Dr. Mary Duncan was our family physician. Except for our Dad — he wouldn't go to her because she was a woman. Robbie was getting funny about it, too.

"Don't be silly." Mom rolled her eyes at Robbie when he objected to his yearly checkup. "Dr. Mary brought you into this world."

She got an appointment for Carrie for the next afternoon.

"Can I come, too?" I asked.

"No. There's no point in both of you missing school."

"Shoot!" I said.

That night Mom happily announced, "Dr. Mary couldn't find a thing wrong with Carrie except she's a little underweight, probably because of the scarlet fever she had in the summer. So she made her up a tonic to take three times a day." She measured the oily brown liquid into a dessert spoon, "Open wide!" she said, and tipped it into Carrie's mouth.

"Ugh!" Carrie jumped up and spit it in the sink. "I don't need a tonic. I feel fine. Why do I have to weigh the same as Connie anyway?"

"Because Dr. Mary and I say so, that's why. Now open your mouth and don't you dare spit it out again."

Carrie gagged down the second lot, knowing Mom meant business.

"Next time," Mom promised, screwing the cap on the bottle, 'I'll mix it with your Ovaltine. That'll make it more palatable."

But Carrie said all it did was spoil our favourite night-time drink.

Well, Dr. Mary's tonic might have tasted terrible, but it worked. The next time we were in the nurse's office, in the middle of December, Carrie had grown half an inch and gained seven pounds. I had stayed the same. We were absolutely identical again.

Chapter 10

Christmas Shopping

It was the Saturday before Christmas. We had finished cleaning our room and were setting the table for lunch.

"Let's go Christmas shopping this aft," I said to Carrie.

Placing the dishes around the poinsettia oilcloth she said, "I promised Ruby I'd go shopping with her."

"With Ruby! What about me?" I grabbed her by the arm. She dropped the teacup she was holding and it broke when it hit the floor.

"Look what you made me do! Mom, look what she made me do!"

"Never mind," Mom said, sipping tomato soup off a wooden spoon to see if it was too spicy. "It was cracked anyway. Sweep it up."

Carrie swept up the china bits and dumped them into the garbage. Then she sulked all through lunch. The minute she was finished, she stomped upstairs. I followed right on her heels.

"What about me?" I repeated.

She pulled open her dresser drawer and rummaged under her socks and knickers (the English word for underpants), looking for her change purse. Sitting on the bottom bunk she began counting her money.

"Five dollars and fifty cents," she said, snapping the purse shut. "Why don't you go with Wendy or Maryanne for a change?"

"I'd rather go with you," I said in a whiny voice.

Carrie looked determined. "Well, if you must know," she said, "I'm going shopping for your present. This year I want to find something truly original, and I want Ruby's advice."

"Oh, okay," I said. "I'll go call for Maryanne."

Neither Maryanne nor Wendy was home so I went by myself. I must have shopped for hours on Jefferson Street but I couldn't find anything I liked. I was just leaning on a telephone pole at the bus-stop when a downtown bus came along. So I hopped on, put a dime in the fare box, and got a seat by the window.

I really enjoyed the ride downtown, looking out at the Christmas lights twinkling in store windows. The bus stopped right in front of the swinging doors of Crowley's Department Store. I had never been there by myself before. It made me feel grown up.

I spent the first hour admiring the store's glorious decorations. Giant Christmas trees were everywhere, glittering with multi-coloured lights. In the toy department I watched the little kids sitting on Santa Claus's lap. I sighed, remembering when I believed in him. Then I asked the floorwalker where the girls' wear was. He told me the fourth floor so I rode up on a crowded elevator.

"Girls' wear, ages 8 to 14!" announced the elevator

operator as she clanked open the folding gates with her white-gloved hand. "Watch your step!"

I sauntered around between the racks of clothes looking at price tags. Uh-oh, I thought. This must be a ritzy store. I guess I should have gone to the Five and Dime. I only had five dollars and ten cents in my pocket.

"May I help you, Miss?" A sweet-faced lady peered at me over a rack of velveteen dresses. Her smile reminded me of my mother's.

"I want to buy my sister something special because we're twins," I explained. "But I've only got five dollars."

"I think I know the very thing," she said. She went behind a counter and came back with a beautiful pink sweater, whip-stitched around the neck in white angora. (I recognized the whip-stitch because I had had to learn it in Home Economics.)

"Are you and your twin identical?" asked the saleslady.

"Yes," I answered proudly.

"Well, why don't you try it on so you'll see how it will look on your sister."

"That's a swell idea," I said. "You see we're mirror twins so when I look in the mirror it's like looking at her instead of me."

"That's a new one on me," she laughed, then she showed me into a dressing-room.

I pulled the pink sweater over my head and looked at myself in the mirror. There was Carrie staring out at me with her gold-speckled green eyes.

I paid the lady and she put it in a red box. Then she slipped it into a Crowley's shopping bag.

It was starting to get dark when I came out of the

store. I felt for my bus fare. One pocket was empty so I felt in the other one. It was empty, too, and it had a hole in it. Frantically I felt the lining of my coat. Nothing. Panic lodged in my throat like a stone. What should I do? I didn't have a nickel to phone home. And even if I did, it would only make Dad mad to have to come all the way downtown in Boris Karloff to get me. I wasn't supposed to be downtown alone.

Could I walk all the way home? It had taken nearly an hour to get downtown by bus. It was too far and too cold to walk. Tears began to fill my eyes. If only Carrie was with me!

Whirling around I pushed the revolving doors and stumbled back inside, almost bumping into the floor-walker. "The store is closing, now, Miss," he said. "You'll have to come back on Monday."

"But . . . but . . ."

"No buts," he said shoving me toward the doors. Then I saw her, the nice saleslady who smiled like my mother. I grabbed her coat just as she was getting swept outside.

"Excuse me!" I cried.

She turned around and when she recognized me she smiled. "Is there something wrong, dear?" she said, and the kindness in her voice made the stone in my throat crack up into tears. Drawing me aside, she asked, "Can I help you?"

"Oh, I hope so." I dashed the tears away with my fist. "I thought I had another dime for bus fare home but I can't find it. I think it fell out a hole in my pocket . . . see . . ." I pulled the pocket inside-out and showed her. "I don't know how I'll get home."

"Well, what if I give you a dime and we call it a Christmas present?" She opened her purse and pressed the coin in my hand.

"Oh, thank you. But I'll pay it back."

Snapping her purse shut she looked up. "Oh, there's my ride," she said. She glanced over her shoulder and cried, "Don't pay it back, dear, pass it on. Merry Christmas!"

"Merry Christmas!" I cried. "Thank you."

* * *

It was completely dark as I hurried up Newport Street. I saw Mom's and Carrie's faces at the window.

"Where have you been?" Mom grabbed the front of my coat and pulled me in the door. "Carrie and I have been worried sick about you."

Carrie shot me a mad look. "You're just lucky Dad isn't home yet," she said. I sighed with relief.

"I'm sorry, Mom," I said. I took off my coat and hat and hung them on the hall coat tree. Then I poured out the whole story. "And the nice saleslady said, 'Don't pay it back, dear, pass it on.' What did she mean by that, Mom? Do you know?"

She gazed up at the ceiling as if searching for the right words. "Well, if you give something away, and don't expect to get it back, the person you gave it to is more likely to help the next person in need. Do you understand Connie?"

"I think so . . . like . . . if I give the blind man who stands in the doorway of the bank with a tin cup . . . if I give him a dime, then maybe he'll share it with somebody else? Is that what it means?"

"We-e-l-l . . ." Mom paused. "Something like that. But

it doesn't have to be money. It can be a loving smile or a kind word or a helping hand just at the right moment." All of a sudden her blue eyes went dreamy. "I just remembered something my Grandma Conroy used to say about that very thing. She called it 'forging a love chain.' When you pass it on, she used to say, you become a link in the love chain."

"Hey! Isn't that who I'm named after, your Grandma Conroy?"

"That's right, and you're well named if I do say so myself."

Carrie had been sitting there quietly, just listening. "Gee, I'm sorry I missed that adventure," she said.

"Too bad for you," I couldn't resist saying.

"Well." Mom gave me one of her eye-rolls. "I'll forgive you this time. But don't ever go downtown alone again."

"I won't," I promised, then I ran upstairs to wrap my present.

Chapter 11

Christmas Day

The thing I liked best about Christmas was that it was the same every year. Red and green paper-chains criss-crossed the living-room ceiling, and our tree sat in its usual corner dressed in the same old decorations. Presents were piled up underneath it, tantalizing us as we waited until it was time to open them.

Mom was in the kitchen checking on the goose. The delicious smell filled the whole house, upstairs and down, because it had been in the oven since six o'clock in the morning. We had roast goose instead of turkey in our house because it reminded Mom of her childhood back in Nottingham, England. And we ate our Christmas dinner at noon instead of suppertime because it was an English tradition.

"It's un-American, eating Christmas dinner at noon-hour," Dad grumbled as he tucked into his huge plate of steaming food.

"Well, this family is only half American," Mom said,

putting a scoop of savory stuffing on her plate. "The other half is British."

"I thought you were Canadian, Dad," Jimmy said, holding a glistening drumstick in both hands.

"I was born in Canada and proud of it; but now I'm a naturalized American and proud of that, too." Dad made a well in his mashed turnip and filled it with golden brown gravy. "Now your mother there, she's still a British subject. She has to go to City Hall every year and register as an alien. Which makes her a foreigner if you ask me."

"Are you really a foreigner, Mom?" asked Robbie, stripping dark meat off the other drumstick.

"I suppose so," Mom admitted with a shrug.

"Then what the heck are we?" Carrie and I said.

"Every last one of you is red-blooded American because you had the good sense to be born right here under the star-spangled banner," Dad said.

Mom rolled her eyes. "Oh, let's stop all the nonsense and enjoy our dinner," she said. "And be sure to leave plenty of room for my English plum pudding."

Another one of our strange family traditions was not to open our presents until after our noonday Christmas dinner. All the other American families we knew opened their presents the minute they got up in the morning. Ruby and Roy Butternick said they sometimes got up in the middle of the night to open theirs. But we liked our own tradition. It made Christmas Day last longer.

Every year each of us kids got something we really needed; this year it was snow boots and fleecy jackets and mitts. But we also got a special surprise. It was usually the toy or game we had asked Santa Claus for. But this year even Jimmy, who would be ten in January, hadn't asked for a toy. He had asked for, and got, a chemistry set.

"Try not to blow us all to kingdom come," Dad joked.

Robbie got his heart's desire: a guitar. Robbie was musical and he made up songs right out of his head.

"Promise not to rupture our eardrums with that thing," Dad snickered.

Carrie and I got a wonderful present, too: a Sears Roebuck hair dryer that you sat under just like in a beauty shop. Now we wouldn't have to stick our heads in the oven after washing our hair anymore.

Dad loved the argyle socks Mom had knitted him and she pretended to be pleased with Dad's gift: a set of Melmac non-scratch dishes. Then it was our turn, Carrie's and mine. We always waited until last to open each other's presents. It was our special twin tradition.

My present was wrapped in green tissue paper and tied with a red bow. Hers was in red paper with a green bow. Dad and Mom leaned forward in their chairs. The trick was to open them at exactly the same time so we would see them at exactly the same time.

"Ready, set, go!" Dad cried and we tore off the bow and paper. The boxes were exactly the same size, but one said Crowley's and the other said J.L. Hudson.

"Ready, set, go!" Dad cried again and we flung the lids in the air.

Squealing with excitement, we each held up our identical pink sweaters with white angora whip-stitching.

"They did it again!" cried Mom, clapping her hands in delight.

Every year Carrie and I tried to surprise each other, and every year we ended up buying the same thing.

"It's beautiful!" I cried, holding the sweater up in

front of me. "Let's wear them to Auntie Sylvia's tonight."

Sylvia Murdock was our mother's best friend but she wasn't really our aunt. We just called her that out of respect. Part of our holiday tradition was to go to her house Christmas night for a slice of her good-luck fruit-cake.

Carrie carefully refolded her sweater and put it back in the Crowley's box. "I'm going to save mine for Ruby's party," she said.

"Ruby's party?" It was the first I'd heard of it.

"It's not till next Saturday," she explained, closing the lid. "She and Roy will be twelve then."

"Aren't I invited too?"

"Oh, sure. Ruby told me to tell you."

I wondered why she hadn't told me earlier.

Chapter 12

Two Different People

We bought Ruby and Roy a Monopoly game because Mom said it would suit them both. It used up our whole week's allowance.

We were really excited because it would be our first mixed party. So far we had only been allowed to go to girl parties. But since Ruby and Roy were girl-and-boy twins Mom and Dad made an exception.

On the day of the party we did each other's hair up in big brush rollers and took turns under the dryer. Then we took turns in the bathroom. I was ready first so I sat on the couch, all dressed up in my pleated blue skirt (Aunt Sylvia had given us identical blue skirts for Christmas) and my angora-trimmed pink sweater, waiting for Carrie.

When she came downstairs you could have knocked me over with a daisy. Her sweater had magically changed from pink to red! And it was trimmed in black instead of white angora.

"That's not the sweater I gave you!" I screeched.

She started putting on her coat. "Oh, I decided to exchange it," she said, not looking at me. "Ruby says red suits me better than pink."

"But . . . but . . . now we aren't identical!" I was boiling mad. "And how could red suit you when it doesn't suit me?"

"Well, Ruby said we should try to look different for a change."

"Well, you can tell Ruby Butternick she's a big buttinski. And if you care so much what she thinks then you can go to her stupid party without me."

I stomped past her up the stairs and turned around halfway. "And you owe me fifty cents for half the present, too."

"Connie . . ." Mom stood at the bottom of the stairs with her hands clasped over the newel post. "You're not being a very good sport about this. After all, Carrie has a right to dress how she pleases."

"And I have a right not to go to the darn party." I ran the rest of the way up the stairs so they wouldn't see me crying.

* * *

I was in bed pretending to be asleep when Carrie came home from the party. I overheard her telling Mom that they had played records and danced with boys. Then Carrie came upstairs, undressed quietly and crept into her bunk.

I started to snore, softly, like a kitten purring. I kept it up about five minutes until all of a sudden I felt a thump in the small of my back. It was Carrie's foot.

"Is there a cat up there?" she whispered.

I kept right on snoring so she gave a hard kick that

made the springs in my bunk go *boing!*

Popping my head over the rail I snapped, "Stop it or I'll come down there and smack you." We had never hit each other in our whole life so I was as surprised as she was to hear myself saying that.

Jumping out of bed she clicked on the ceiling light. Then she came over and rested her chin on the rail of my bunk. I stared straight up at the ceiling.

"Connie . . ."

I didn't answer.

"Connie . . ." Her voice had a little tremor in it. "It's just that I want to be an individual for a change."

I swung my head sideways so fast I got a crick in my neck. "Why don't you say what you mean . . . that you don't want to be twins anymore," I snapped.

"That's not what I mean. We'll always be twins. And you'll always be my best friend . . . but . . ."

"But you don't want to look like me."

"No! That's not it either. Most of the time I want to be us, having fun fooling everybody. But . . ."

I shoved up on my elbows, "But what?"

"But I want to be myself . . . not part of you. Haven't you ever felt like being just Connie Taylor, instead of half of 'the twins'? Just yesterday the gas-meter man asked me was I twin number one or twin number two."

"What did you say?"

"I just gave him a dirty look."

I flopped back on my boingy springs. It was the first time I'd ever really thought about it. That we were two different people.

Myself. Herself. I had always imagined that when we grew up, we'd have twins just like us and we'd all live together in the same house. This house because Mom and Dad would probably be dead by then. I hadn't bothered to imagine husbands. But now I did. If we married, we'd have different names. We would live in different houses. On different streets. What if Carrie and her husband went to live in a different city? What if her children were boys and mine were girls?

Carrie clicked off the light and crept back into bed. Then she started singing quietly,

Once I had a secret love
That lived within the heart of me
All too soon my secret love
Became impatient to be free . . .

Turning toward the wall, I squeezed my eyes shut to hold back the tears. I wished I had gone to the party after all.

Chapter 13

Magic In a Box

January blew into February and nothing seemed to change. Every day we slogged to school through frozen slush in our new Christmas boots. Detroit was having a winter of record-breaking cold, the weatherman said on the radio.

Robbie came down with a terrible cold after watching the Detroit Red Wings lose an important hockey game to the Toronto Maple Leafs at the Olympia. Our whole family were Red Wings fans but we didn't get too mad if we lost to the Leafs, because of our Toronto connection.

At first Robbie thought his throat hurt from cheering, but it didn't go away. Soon he was croaking like a bullfrog. Mom made him mustard plasters, and he had to sit under a towel-tent inhaling steam from a basin of boiling water laced with Friar's Balsam. Then it turned out that it wasn't just a bad cold Robbie had, it was the Asian flu and it laid him up for five whole weeks.

Doctor Duncan came every day and she said the rest of us kids had to keep our distance because Robbie was contagious. So Jimmy had to move downstairs onto the living-room sofa and us twins couldn't even put our heads in his door. Near the end of his isolation Robbie started to rebel. "I'm bored crazy up here!" he bellowed loud enough for the whole neighbourhood to hear.

"Oh-oh." Mom rolled her eyes to the ceiling. "Your brother's on the mend. He's exactly like your father when he's nearly better, cantankerous as a bear."

"I'm starving up here!" croaked Robbie. And Mom gave her head a worried little shake. "I still hear that frog in his throat," she said.

Loading up Robbie's supper tray with beef broth, hot biscuits and green Jell-O, Mom said to Carrie and me, "It's time you twins set the table."

I climbed up on the step-stool to get the non-scratch dishes down. They were covered in scratches already. While I shuffled the plates onto the new green-checkered oilcloth, Carrie placed the cutlery around them.

"The sharp side of the knife is supposed to be turned in," I said.

"Well, Mrs. Butternick turns them out," Carrie said. "And she puts the spoons beside the plates, not across the top like we do."

"Oh, what does she know," I scoffed.

Just then Mom came down. She took one look at the table and started to rearrange the cutlery. "If there's anything we English know," she said, "it's how to lay a proper table."

I was just about to say "I told you so" when we heard Boris Karloff's horn blaring out the front.

"Dad's home," cried Jimmy, running to the door.

He flung it open and a current of cold air flowed down the hall into the kitchen.

"Close the door! You're cooling off my supper!" cried Mom, clattering dinner plates on top the steaming bowls.

Then Jimmy let out a piercing shriek that brought us all scurrying to the front hall.

Up the veranda steps staggered our dad, leaning backward to keep his balance, his nose red as a cherry. In his arms he carried a huge cardboard box.

"Make way!" he cried, laughter in his voice. Then he stumbled in the door and lowered the box, with a loud grunt, onto the hall runner.

On top of the box in scrawly handwriting someone had written: "Fragile, this side up." On the front of the box printed in big black letters was the word Motorola.

"MOTOROLA!"

Shrieking with glee Carrie and I grabbed each other by the hands and danced around in circles. "It's television! Television! Television!" we screamed.

Jimmy yelled up the stairs, "Robbie! Robbie! Dad's got us a television!" Robbie was already hanging over the bannister.

Dad snapped open his penknife and began sawing through the tape that sealed the box.

Mom stood there frowning and twisting her apron into a roll. "Can we afford it?" she asked doubtfully.

Dad shrugged and closed his penknife. "Well, Ira Wattles — you know that skinny fella with the big Adam's apple beside me on the line? Well, he got it for me wholesale from his brother-in-law who's in the business; and he says it's the best television on the market." Folding back the cardboard flaps, he ran his hand across the top of the walnut cabinet. "And I thought it might help Robbie recuperate," he added.

"Oh!" Mom dropped her apron. "What a perfect excuse."

Then Dad ripped open the front of the box and rolled the Motorola (a floor model on wheels!) through the French doors and across the living-room carpet. Mom hurried past him and whisked away an occasional chair to make a space in the corner.

Stretched across the blank screen was a wide red ribbon with shiny gold letters which read: "Giant 17-inch screen."

"Turn it on! Turn it on!" screamed Carrie and I.

"You got to plug it in first, stupids," scoffed Jimmy, untwisting the cord.

"You can plug it in all you like but it won't work without an aerial," Dad said.

* * *

We had to wait two whole days for the men to come and climb up on our roof and attach an apparatus to our chimney that looked like the spokes of a giant umbrella. Then Mom wouldn't let us touch the television set until Dad came home from work.

We were all lined up on the sofa, like dolls on a shelf, waiting for the big moment. Robbie was cocooned in a blanket on Dad's La-Z-Boy in the farthest corner of the room, in case he was still contagious.

"You ready?" Dad asked Mom.

"Ready!" she said, her finger on the lamp-switch.

Simultaneously, Dad pressed the television's 'on' button and Mom switched off the light. But nothing happened. We were sitting in the dark.

"Is it broke already?" cried Jimmy.

"It takes time to warm up," Dad said. But he didn't sound too sure.

Then, softly, like morning light coming in the window, the screen began to glow. And there, on the magic box, in our very own living room, was a moving, talking picture.

"Ohhhh!" Our sighs filled the room

"Isn't it wonderful!" marvelled Mom.

"Super-duper!" Carrie and I cried.

"Black and white and crystal clear!" crowed our dad, proud as a peacock. "You'll never see a better picture on the face of the globe, I'll guarantee."

Chapter 14

Television Madness

We could get four stations on our Motorola. ("Channels," Robbie corrected, "not stations.") And Dad said if we had a rotator attached to the aerial we could probably even get Canada.

Robbie recovered like magic while watching television. For a while he even stopped strumming his guitar. He started a little notebook in which he wrote down every single program and the names of the stars and the exact time that every show came on the air. Then he printed on the cover: "Rob Taylor's Television Tips."

For several weeks Carrie forgot all about "individuating." We were all television crazy. We'd watch absolutely anything just so long as it talked and moved. At lunchtime we'd race home, grab our sandwiches off the counter, and park on the carpet to watch *Search For Tomorrow*. It was a soap-box story that Mom had listened to for years on the radio. But we weren't interested in it until it came to life on our giant 17-inch screen.

After supper the dishes would fly out of the dish pan with bits of food still clinging to the plates. And Mom would plop them right back in again. "The more hurry the less speed," she'd say in a sing-songy voice.

"But *The Lone Ranger* . . ." I began.

" . . . will be on in five minutes!" Carrie finished.

"Then you'd better get a move on," was Mom's maddening reply.

Saturday nights, we got to stay up to watch *Your Show of Shows*. When it ended, we'd beg to stay up just a little longer, so that we could watch the test pattern.

Jimmy and Carrie and I got in the habit of sitting on the fringe of the carpet with our noses not six inches from the screen. So one night Dad brought home a lamp shaped like a green panther. He put it on top of the walnut cabinet and plugged it in. The light shone backward on the wall. "It's called indirect lighting," Dad explained to Mom who was wrinkling her nose at the green panther. "Ira Wattles' brother-in-law recommended it. He said it prevents foolish children who sit too close to the screen from going blind." So Mom sighed and accepted it because she didn't want us to go blind.

* * *

One day Carrie and I were late getting home from school because we had had to stay in after three-thirty to finish our homework. Throwing our book bags on the sofa we parked ourselves on the fringe of the carpet.

Robbie, who hadn't started back to school yet, was watching television from Dad's La-Z-Boy. I glanced at the anniversary clock on the mantle. It was called that because Dad had given it to Mom on their first anniversary. It was a tall glass tube with three gold balls that twirled back and forth. It said four-thirty.

"Whew! Just in time!" said Carrie, and I leaned forward and cranked the knob to change the channel.

"Hey!" Robbie bellowed. "I'm watching my cowboy show!"

"Well, we have to see *Cisco Kid*," Carrie and I cried.

Bouncing out of the La-Z-Boy like a rubber ball, Robbie cracked his knuckles on both our heads and cranked the knob back to his show.

We let out a blood-curdling scream as Mom came tripping down the stairs with an armload of laundry.

"What is it? What's the matter?" she cried.

"The darn twins turned off my program," grumbled Robbie.

"He's making us miss *Cisco*," wailed Carrie.

"And he hit us on our noggins," I complained, rubbing my head.

"Robbitson!" — that made us snicker — "You must never hit your sisters on their heads. It could damage their brains."

"Huh!" snorted Robbie. "Probably be an improvement."

"I want to watch *Cisco*, too!" Jimmy plunked himself down, cross-legged, between us.

"Majority rules!" we squealed and cranked back to *Cisco*.

"We-e-l-l," Mom wagged her finger at Robbie, "since you lost your temper and hit the twins . . ."

"That's not fair! They had it coming." Picking up his notebook of television tips, Robbie stomped away upstairs.

"From now on you'll have to learn to negotiate," Mom said.

"I can't put up with all the arguing." Shaking her head, she turned on her heel and the rubber lift of her house shoe squeaked on the hardwood floor as she headed for the kitchen.

From upstairs we could hear Robbie strumming his guitar and singing in a cowboy voice: "Rolling along like a tumbling tumble weed!"

Jimmy got up and shut the French doors.

Carrie and I had won that round. But it was the beginning of a big family feud. The only thing we ever agreed on was Ed Sullivan on Sunday nights. It was a variety show (Ed pronounced it "shew") with comics and dancers and acrobats and singers.

"What a marvellous show," Mom breathed as it ended.

"The man's a stumble-bum," Dad declared. "I could do better sitting on my thumbs." (Dad's favourite show was *Father Knows Best*.) Pushing on the footrest, he popped himself out of the La-Z-Boy and snapped off the set.

"Yeah, me too," agreed Robbie.

"When I grow up . . ." said Jimmy, his big, blue eyes filled with wonder, "I'm going to have a magic show like that guy." He pointed at the empty screen where, just minutes before, a magician had pulled a pigeon right out of a hat; now, all that was left was a white dot of light slowly shrinking in the middle of the black screen. Then it blinked and went out like a fallen star.

Chapter 15

Double Trouble

One Monday afternoon I straggled home late from school with a note from Miss Markle in my book bag. I had gotten caught without my homework done. I took my book bag upstairs and stashed it under the bed.

Robbie had beat me to the T.V. again but I wasn't going to fight about it. "Can I look at your 'Television Tips'?" I asked him. "I want to see what's on tonight." He threw his notebook at me and I caught it on the fly.

I studied his descriptions of the shows: Wild Western, Dynamic Drama, Crazy Comedy. And I studied something else: Robbie's handwriting was almost exactly like our dad's.

I tossed him back his notebook and watched as Roy Rogers ambled through the sagebrush on his horse, Trigger, strumming his guitar and singing in his stringy voice, "There's a love-knot in my lariat."

"You can play the guitar just as good as him," I told Robbie. "And you can sing even better."

"Thanks," he said with a surprised grin.

Mom poked her head into the living room. "Where's Carrie?" she asked.

"Oh, she and Ruby Butternick volunteered to help Mr. Bradley clean the blackboards and bang the chalk out of the brushes," I said.

A short time later Carrie came in the front door and caught my eye. She jerked her head toward the stairs, giving me the high sign. So I followed her.

Shutting our bedroom door we sat on the bottom bunk. "What's up?" I whispered.

"I've got a note from my teacher for Mom and Dad," she said, and she pulled a sealed envelope out of her book bag.

"So have I." I pulled the exact same envelope out of my book bag.

"Let's open them," suggested Carrie.

"Okay. They won't know they're supposed to be in envelopes."

The contents of the notes were almost identical. "Caroline's marks are slipping badly and I am concerned. She has been lax with her homework lately. I thought you should be made aware of the situation. Sincerely, Thomas Bradley," read Carrie. Then it was my turn.

"Conroy's marks are sliding down scale and I am disappointed. Also, her homework has been late in completion. I thought you should know. Sincerely, Marlene Markle."

"Mom will be mad as hops," Carrie said.

"Dad will kill us," I said.

"What'll we do?" we both said. We were silent. I thought: Do we dare?

62

"I've got an idea," I said.

"What?" she whispered hopefully.

So I told her what I had in mind, and she thought it was a great idea. We were in cahoots again! I went to the top of the stairs and called in a really nice voice, "Robbie, will you come up here for a minute?"

"What for?" He sounded reasonably friendly.

"We need you to fix something."

That always worked with Robbie because he liked fixing things. We shut the door behind him and let him read the notes from our teachers.

"What do you expect me to do about it?" he asked skeptically.

"Well . . . I noticed in your 'Television Tips' that your writing is just like Dad's. And I thought maybe you could write a note and say we both promise to work harder . . . something like that."

"And forge Dad's name?"

Carrie and I exchanged glances. "Well . . . yes," we said.

"What's in it for me?" he asked slyly.

"What do you want?"

"Got any money?"

We pulled open a dresser drawer and got out a pair of folded socks, our newest hiding-place from Jimmy. We unfolded the socks and out fell two orange two-dollar bills. Uncle Emery had given them to us last summer. We soon found out you couldn't spend Canadian money in Detroit so we were saving them for our next visit to Toronto.

"I'll take them," Robbie said, and he snatched the bills and put them in his pocket.

I gave him a writing pad and Carrie handed him the

ballpoint pen that Ruby had given her for Christmas. It had clear liquid inside of it and a teeny-weeny boat floated back and forth on teeny-weeny waves.

"Nice pen," Robbie said. "I'll take it too."

"Greedy-guts!" we grumbled.

"Quit talking like parrots. Do you want me to write the notes or not?"

We clamped our mouths shut and nodded our heads.

* * *

Robbie's writing would have fooled a handwriting expert. Our teachers swallowed the notes hook, line and sinker. We thought we were home free. For another whole week we didn't do a lick of homework. And Mom and Dad didn't even notice because they were mesmerized by the magic box, too.

So, sure enough, the following Friday night we twins came home with another note from our teachers. This time they were worded even more seriously.

"What'll we do now?" we asked each other.

"The same as before I guess," we answered.

We had to wait until Robbie came home from high school. He was late because he had football practice that night.

"I don't like him playing football," Mom said, glancing anxiously at the cuckoo clock. "I remember when I was in middle school, back in England, and a boy in my class got hit on the head in a rugby game. He had concussion and his brain swelled up and he was never the same again."

Mom was always worrying about our brains!

We met Robbie at the front door and herded him up the stairs.

He grinned as he read the notes. "How much is it worth this time?" he asked greedily.

We had no idea, before all this happened, how mercenary our big brother was. "I've got fifty cents left from my allowance," I said.

"I've only got a quarter," Carrie said.

"I'll take it," said Greedy-guts.

He had the first note written and had started on the second when all of a sudden the door opened and Dad poked his head in smiling cheerfully. "Your mother has supper ready," he said.

Instinctively Robbie covered the page with his elbow. A red flush crept up his neck and spread across his cheekbones.

The smile disappeared from Dad's face. He stepped in the room and held out his hand. The paper rattled as Robbie handed it to him. On it was written, "Mar. 15, 1954. Dear Mr. Bradley . . ."

Dad's eyes narrowed as he surveyed the room. The note to Miss Markle was lying, naked, on the dresser. He picked it up and read it.

Carrie squeezed my hand so hard I nearly yelped. Robbie sat so still he reminded me of that insect that plays dead and makes itself look like the twig it's sitting on.

Dad carefully creased the note in half, then in quarters, then he put it in his shirt pocket. His voice, when he spoke, was as cold as steel.

"Go to bed, all of you!" he ordered. Then he turned on his heel and trod heavily down the stairs.

We caught Robbie's shirtsleeves as he headed toward the door. "Give us back our money," we hissed.

Brushing us off as if we were pesky flies he hissed back, "Try and get it," and left the room.

We lay awake for hours that night. We heard Mom and Dad come up to bed but they weren't talking to each other like they usually did.

My stomach was rumbling from emptiness and when I finally did go to sleep I dreamed I was eating a big plateful of pancakes swimming in maple syrup from Quebec, Canada.

Chapter 16

Cruel and Unusual Punishment

It was the worst thing any of us had ever done. Robbie had to give up football practice for two whole weeks. "Every cloud has a silver lining," Mom said, heaving a sigh of relief. As for us twins, we expected the most terrible spanking of our lives — but we didn't get it. That would be too easy, Dad said. Instead we were barred from watching television until Easter. And it was only the middle of March!

"It's cruel and unusual punishment," Carrie whimpered from the bottom bunk.

"Yeah. I'd rather get spanked and get it over with," I agreed.

Every night after supper, Mom and Dad would send us three up to our rooms. Then, just to torture us, they'd close the French doors, switch on the electric fireplace and the T.V., and turn the volume down so low we couldn't hear it.

Jimmy was allowed to stay up.

"Can't you just see the little brat all cuddled up beside Mom on the sofa?" grumbled Carrie, punching her pillow.

"Yeah. What a disgusting sight," I said. Then I got up to go to the bathroom. When I came out of the bathroom I got down on my hands and knees and crawled to the top of the stairs. Peeking between the bannister posts I could see through the French doors into the living room. The light between the imitation logs in the fireplace danced like real flames. And the black-and-white picture Dad was so proud of flickered enticingly. But I couldn't hear a word. Scared of getting caught, I backed up into our room, quietly shut the door, and climbed the ladder to my bunk.

"What did you see?" whispered Carrie.

"*I Love Lucy*," I whispered back.

"Oh, no! I love that program," she moaned.

"What'll we do to make the time go faster?" I wondered out loud.

Then we both cried, "Homework!"

Every night after that, we'd splash through the dishes and race up the stairs with our book bags and spread our books out on our desk. We were amazed at how fast the time went by when we put our minds to our studies. And our Easter report cards made it all worthwhile.

Mom was delighted. "Six A's and a B!" she exclaimed. "Just wait until your father sees this."

Dad was delighted too. "Good for you," he said, and his praise was music to our ears. "Just for that you can stay up an extra hour, starting Saturday night, and watch television." He looked at us sternly. "Provided your homework is done, of course."

Saturday night we bathed together to save time, jumped into our pj's, and sprawled on the carpet.

Jimmy switched on the Motorola and we waited excitedly for it to warm up. We waited and waited and waited . . . but the screen stayed black as pitch.

"Dad! Dad!" The three of us went clattering down to the cellar, where Dad was fixing a kitchen chair.

"What is it? What's wrong?" he cried in alarm.

"The Motorola! It's broken!"

"Oh, for John's sake!" Dad said. "I thought somebody had got killed. Did you give it time to warm up?"

"It won't warm up," Jimmy said. "It's really broke this time, Dad."

Dad dropped the rung of the chair on his worktable and followed us up the wooden stairs.

The whole family, including our mom, sat dolefully staring at the black screen as Dad took the back off the cabinet and poked around inside.

"A-ha!" he exclaimed, holding up a smoky glass tube. "Just as I thought. I'll be back in a jiffy."

Then he threw on his hat and coat, ran out the door, jumped into Boris Karloff and went backfiring down Newport Street.

"Where's he going?" asked Carrie and I.

Nobody answered so we just sat there waiting. A short time later we heard Boris Karloff chugging back up the street. Then Dad came bursting in the door, grinning from ear to ear. "They've got a machine down at the cigar store called a tube-tester," he beamed. "Sure enough, that's what it was — a burnt-out tube."

Ducking behind the set he popped in a brand new

tube. "Turn it on, Mother!" he ordered.

Mom clicked the 'on' switch and we held our breath. Slowly the screen began to glow and the picture flashed on, just in time for *Your Show of Shows*, starring Sid Caesar and Imogene Coca.

Halfway through the hilarious show Carrie said, "Oh, I wish Ruby was here. She just loves comedies."

"Oh, Ruby-Scuby!" I scoffed.

"Shhhhh!" hissed the rest of the family.

Chapter 17

Individuating Again

The very next Friday night Carrie brought Ruby home. "Mom, this is my best friend, Ruby Butternick. Can she stay for supper?"

Ruby was standing in the doorway anxiously awaiting Mom's reply. The Butternicks didn't have a television yet.

"Well, I don't know. I understand you have a twin brother," Mom said to Ruby. "Won't he be lonely without you?"

"Oh, no!" Ruby shook her thick red Little Orphan Annie curls. "Roy's got lots of friends."

"Boy and girl twins are lucky that way," Carrie explained. "They can individuate."

"I've even got my own room," bragged Ruby.

"Oh, that must be wonderful," gushed Carrie.

I gave them both a dirty look and stomped upstairs.

I always thought Carrie liked sharing bunk beds with me. We used to talk every night and tell each other everything. That's why we got all those spankings. But lately I'd noticed that Carrie would go to sleep while I was still talking.

Jimmy called me for supper and when I came down everybody was already sitting. Ruby was sitting in my place.

I stood right beside her and said, "Excuse me, you're in my chair." But before Ruby could move Mom said, "You sit still, Ruby. Connie, you can sit in your father's place. He's working late tonight." Sitting in Dad's chair mollified me a bit.

We had sausages, which Mom called bangers, and scrambled eggs and hash-brown potatoes.

"I'm not allowed to eat eggs," Ruby said.

"For mercy's sake, why not?" asked Mom.

"They make me itchy."

"Me, too," agreed Carrie.

"They do not!" I snapped at Carrie. "If eggs itched you they'd itch me, too."

Helping herself from the platter, Mom said, "I've never noticed you scratching yourself after eating eggs, Carrie."

"Well, only last week when you gave us egg sandwiches I got a rash on my elbows. So my teacher sent me down to the nurse's office and Miss Christmas put calamine lotion on my elbows and told me not to eat eggs anymore."

Mom rolled her eyes. "Well, that's news to me," she said.

"I'll take yours, then," Jimmy said, and he scraped the scrambled eggs off the platter onto his plate.

After supper Ruby said, "Can we watch T.V. now, Mrs. Taylor?"

Before Mom got a chance to answer I said, "No. Carrie and me have to do the dishes first."

"Well, perhaps tonight we can make an exception," Mom said. "You and your friend can be excused, Carrie. Connie and I will wash up." They scampered into the living room with the boys.

I was fit to be tied. "That's not fair, Mom," I protested. "You've never treated us different before."

Lifting the checkered skirt that was strung around the sink to hide the cleaning stuff Mom got the Lux Flakes off a shelf and the dishpan off a nail. "Well, maybe it's time I did, Connie." Her voice was thoughtful. "I think it would be good for you both to make new friends." She handed me a dishtowel. "You're welcome to bring your friends home, too, you know."

Wiping the soap bubbles off the plate, I thought about Wendy Johnson. Wendy didn't have television at her house either, so maybe she'd like to come sometime. And there was a new girl in class that I sort of liked named Kitty Foxcroft. Maybe I'd ask one of them over.

When the dishes were done I hung up the towel on the spokes above the stove and sauntered into the front room. My twin sister and her best friend — her new best friend, since it used to be me — were squeezed into Dad's La-Z-Boy with their arms around each other and their heads together, giggling. *I Remember Mama* was just coming on. It was one of my favourite shows. But Carrie and Ruby's silliness got on my nerves so bad that I jumped up right in the middle of it and flounced upstairs again.

I wish I had someone to talk to, I thought. I can't talk to Mom or Carrie because they don't understand me anymore. Then I had an idea. I'd start a diary and talk to myself.

I sharpened a pencil and found a brand-new workbook in my book bag. Carrie and I had kept diaries when we were young. We used to compare them and laugh to see that we had both written all the same stuff, almost word for word.

On the front cover, where it said "Subject" I printed in capital letters: CONNIE TAYLOR'S DIARY. PRIVATE PROPERTY. KEEP OUT. Inside I began:

April 3, 1954.

Dear Diary: Today I asked my teacher, Miss Markle, is there any such word as individuate. She said she didn't think so, that I should look it up in my Webster's. It wasn't there. That's what my twin sister, Carrie, says we have to do from now on, individuate. Right now she is downstairs individuating with Ruby Butternick. But I know Carrie better than anybody. I know what she thinks and what she likes and what she hates, because mirror twins are basically the same person. So I'm sure that Carrie will soon get sick of Ruby Butternick because Ruby says everything twice when it wasn't even interesting the first time. When Carrie and I used to talk — before she took sick and her hair got curly (she seemed to change after that) — we had some very deep and stimulating conversations. We even had our own language called Twinnish that nobody else could understand. But we had to stop using it because it got us in trouble. Everybody thought we were talking about them. Also, we used to write in Twinnish and pretty soon we were making mistakes in school because we were forgetting how to spell in English. We haven't used it for months now and I am beginning to forget it. But it proves how much alike we were. Still are if only Carrie would stop trying to "individuate" or whatever the heck she's doing down there with Ruby. I guess I'll have to change, too, but it's going to be hard. Just last night I woke up with a pain in my mouth. I smelled cloves — sure enough, Mom was stuffing a wad of cotton-batting soaked in oil-of-cloves into Carrie's hollow tooth. I just heard the front door shut so I guess Ruby's gone home. I think I'll go down and make myself a peanut-butter sandwich. To be continued . . .

Carrie came out to the kitchen and started making a bologna and mustard sandwich on the counter beside me. "Does peanut butter make you itch, too?" I sneered.

Carrie made a disgusted clicking sound with her tongue. "If you'll stop being sarcastic I'll tell you something funny," she said.

I was so glad she wanted to tell me something that I apologized for being sarcastic. "Go ahead. I'm listening," I said.

"Well, Ruby's —"

"Oh, not Ruby again!"

"No, it's not about Ruby, it's about her twin brother. But if you don't want to hear . . ."

"I want to hear." Jimmy's muffled voice came from inside the Frigidaire. He was halfway in there, rooting around. He came out with a bowl of cold pork-and-beans and started to make himself a bean sandwich.

"Well," Carrie began, "Roy Butternick says that his favourite sandwich is peanut butter and ashes."

"Ashes! What kind of ashes?"

"Cigarette ashes. Mrs. Butternick always has a Camel hanging out of her mouth when she makes their school lunches and ashes get sprinkled on the peanut butter. Ruby hates it but Roy says it gives the sandwich a unique, smoky flavour."

"We should try it sometime," snickered Jimmy.

"Fat chance," Mom said, coming in to brew herself a cup of tea. "I didn't know Mrs. Butternick smoked. What does her husband say?"

"Oh, he just opens the door no matter how cold it is outside and tells Mrs. Butternick the door stays open until she butts out."

"Oh, my!" Mom rolled her eyes. "Do they fight about it?"

"No. They joke about it. They joke about everything at their house."

The more Carrie talked about her friend's family the more jealous I got. The Butternicks sounded like fun.

"Maybe I could come with you next time you're invited over there," I suggested.

"No! You find your own friend," Carrie objected. "How are we ever going to individuate if you go everywhere I go?"

"Stop using that stupid word," I snapped. "Miss Markle says it doesn't even exist."

"It does too exist. Just because she's a teacher doesn't mean she knows everything."

"Well, she knows more than you do!"

"Stop it!" Mom swiped the crumbs off the counter with the dishcloth. "I'm surprised at you two. You never bickered like this before, and I won't stand for it now."

That night while I was in the bathroom Carrie found my diary. When I came back in the bedroom I caught her reading it. Snatching it out of her hands I yelled, "Can't you read?" I pointed to the capital letters on the cover. "It says PRIVATE PROPERTY!"

"Oh, don't get your shirt in a knot." That sounded like a smart-alecky saying she had picked up from the Butternicks. "I know what you're thinking anyway."

I couldn't help but grin when she said that, and I instantly stopped being mad. Climbing into my bunk, I leaned over the bar. "Ginny-winny-ninny-gite!" I said.

"Ginny-winny-ninny-gite!" she replied.

We hadn't forgotten Twinnish after all.

Chapter 18

Kitty Foxcroft

"My mother says you can come to supper anytime you like, Wendy." Wendy Johnson and Kitty Foxcroft and me were walking home together. "You, too, Kitty," I added.

Wendy's pale blue eyes lit up for a minute, then the light faded and went out. "I don't think I can," she said. "My mother never lets me go anywhere."

"Why not?" asked Kitty, her brown eyes glittering with curiosity. It was easy to tell that Kitty was a nosey-parker.

"I . . . I . . . I . . ." Wendy stuttered when she was nervous. "I c–c–can't t–t–tell you," she said.

We stopped in front of Wendy's house, just two doors up from mine, and there was her mother standing in the doorway hugging herself in a sweater. "Wendy, you come in here!" she cried in a shrill voice. "I don't want you dilly-dallying out on the street."

Wendy ran up the walk without even saying goodbye and her mother gave her a little shove into the house and shut the door.

"I heard Wendy's mother is . . . you know." Kitty

twirled her finger in circles around her ear. Then she added quickly, "But I can come to your house any time I want to. All I have to do is tell my mother."

"Well . . . okay." I would rather have had Wendy but I guessed Kitty was better than nobody.

Mom said, sure, Kitty could stay, just so long as she liked Yorkshire pudding. That was another one of Mom's English dishes that she made to remind her of the "old country."

"I like everything," Kitty said. Then she phoned her mother and got permission to stay.

We were in the living room watching Howdy Doody when Robbie came in the front hall with Arthur Pool, Betty Pool's brother. Kitty craned her neck and stared at them through the French doors.

"Who's that?" she said in an excited whisper.

"Oh, it's just my brother, Robbie, and the boy next door."

"He's cute," mewed Kitty.

"Who?"

"Both. It must be swell to have a cute brother who brings home cute boys." Kitty started fluffing up her hair and pinching her cheeks and biting her lips.

All through supper, and after supper, too, while we were watching television, Kitty kept making goo-goo eyes at the boys. Especially Robbie. At first he grinned at her, but after a while he got sick of her and signalled Arthur to follow him upstairs.

"Are they coming back?" whispered Kitty, watching them disappear.

"No." I said. Then I thought, And neither are you.

Next time I would try to get Wendy to come. If I had

to individuate I'd rather do it with her — I was pretty sure that Wendy wouldn't act silly over boys. Maybe I'd ask my mom to phone her mom. That might work.

* * *

Carrie and I got on swell that week, talking in Twinnish and having fun together. She seemed to have forgotten all about individuating. Then on Friday I waited for her in the schoolyard until I was the only kid left. Mr. Morganstern, our principal, came out the double front doors pulling on his gloves.

"What are you doing still here, Conroy?" he asked me. I was surprised and embarrassed that he knew my real name.

"I'm waiting for my twin sister, Sir," I said. I always mentioned that we were twins because I thought that made the waiting sound more imperative.

"Well, there's nobody left in the school so you'd better be on your way," he said.

It wasn't like Carrie to disappear without telling me, so I ran all the way home and burst in the kitchen door. "Where's Carrie?" I asked Mom breathlessly. "I waited for her after school but she never came."

"Oh, she just telephoned to say that she had gone home with Ruby." Taking a starched dress out of her dampening bag, she fitted it over the ironing board.

"Is she staying there for supper again?" I asked.

"Well, ye-e-s," she said, ironing steadily.

The way she dragged out the e's made me suspicious.

"How long is she going to stay?"

"We-e-l-l-l . . ." Now she was dragging out the l's. "Ruby's mother has invited her to stay overnight."

"Overnight! We hate sleeping in strange beds."

"There's a special reason this time."

"What is it?"

"The Butternicks are moving to San Bernardino, California and that means Carrie and Ruby won't be seeing each other for a long time. Perhaps never. So Mrs. Butternick thought it might be nice if they spent their last weekend together."

I could hardly keep the grin off my face. That night I wrote in my diary:

> *April 20, 1954.*
>
> *Dear Diary: I've decided to be extra nice to Carrie from now on, so she won't go looking for another best friend when Ruby's gone. That's why I was so jealous of Ruby — because Carrie called her her best friend. I'll stay friends with Wendy Johnson, of course, but not best friends. That's the key word — best. Poor Wendy can only have school friends anyway, not after-school friends. Wendy is an only child and her mother will not let her out of her sight. One day Wendy told me why. It was because her brother, William, got killed by lightning on Lake St. Clair while he was fishing with their father. Mr. Johnson tried to save his son but he couldn't. Then after that he went away and was never seen again. So Wendy is all Mrs. Johnson's got left and she said she would die if she lost her, too. So Wendy says she is trapped. She says she feels like a prisoner of love.*
>
> *Hmm, I wonder if Carrie feels a bit like that. Not that she's a prisoner of love or anything, but I must admit I think I'd die without her. To be continued . . .*

Chapter 19

Our Twelfth Birthday

"What sort of party would you like this year?" Mom asked.

May 16th would be our twelfth birthday and it was exactly two weeks away. Because it was Mom's birthday, too, we used to have strictly family parties. But the year we turned ten she let us have our own party.

"Mixed!" we yelled.

"Oh, I don't know about mixed," Mom rolled her eyes and laughed. "Your dad might not agree to that. Why don't you just have all your special friends. You can play parlour games and I'll make fish and chips." Mom loved fish and chips because she was English.

"Ruby had a mixed party . . ." Carrie started to say.

" . . . and her dad didn't mind." I finished.

"What's this about a party?" Dad came up from the cellar smelling of turpentine. He went to the sink and sudsed up his hands with carbolic soap.

"Carrie and me want a mixed party for our birthday, Dad. That should be okay because we'll be entering our thirteenth year."

"Which means you're just about to turn twelve," Dad said. "So mixed is out. Unless, of course, your brothers are invited too."

Jimmy yelled from the living room. "Do I have to give a present if I come to their party?"

"NO, because you're not coming!" we yelled back.

"Make a list," Mom said. Handing Dad a towel off the rack she shook Dutch Cleanser into the sink and started scrubbing.

I put Wendy at the top of my list. "Will you phone Wendy's mother, Mom? She might not let her come if I ask her."

"For mercy's sake, why not?" asked Mom.

"She can't go anywhere because her brother, William, got killed by lightning."

"Lightning!" cried Mom and Dad and Carrie.

"Lightning!" Jimmy came running from the living room.

So I explained to everybody what had happened to Wendy's brother and father. "And now Wendy can't go anywhere except school. But if you phone Mrs. Johnson, Mom, maybe she'll let her come."

"Well, I'll certainly do my best," Mom said.

Carrie was making her list on Mom's grocery pad. I leaned over and took a quick glance at it. The first name on her list was Pamela Potter.

"Who's Pamela Potter?" I asked suspiciously. I'd never heard that name before.

"She's a new girl in my class," Carrie said. "They just moved here from Traverse City. I really like her. We have a lot in common."

The hair on the back of my neck started to prickle.

"Like what?" I snapped.

"Oh, lots of things," Carrie answered with a shrug.

"Go ahead with your list, Connie," Mom suggested, "And I'll ring up Mrs. Johnson."

We were allowed to invite five kids each, which, including us, made twelve. The number of kids at our party always matched our age.

* * *

The day of our party Robbie took Jimmy to the movies. All the girls were disappointed. Not about Jimmy — about Robbie.

Wendy was allowed to come. She was the only one not dressed up. She was wearing her old school-dress, but it was clean.

Instead of fish and chips, Mom served hot dogs, potato chips and root beer. For dessert there were two pink-iced birthday cakes with twelve multi-coloured candles on each, and four bricks of raspberry-ripple ice cream.

After the repast (even though the food was American, Mom still used her English word) we opened our presents.

I got a box of handkerchiefs, a pair of blue barrettes, a celluloid comb-and-brush set, and two boxes of stationery. Carrie got a box of chocolate-covered cherries, two autograph books, an apron, and a string of red glass beads.

"Oh, thank you, Pam!" Carrie gushed, holding the sparkling red beads up against her new white chiffon party dress. The chiffon party dresses were presents from Mom and Dad.

"I just knew red was your colour," smirked Pam as she fastened them around Carrie's neck.

"I hate red," I said.

Mom gave me a warning tap on the head with her wedding ring.

"Would you girls prefer to play party games or watch television?" she asked.

"Television!" everybody cried, because most of their houses didn't have T.V. sets yet. It was a good night for television, starting with The Lone Ranger.

Later, when we were getting ready for bed, I asked Carrie what her favourite present was.

"The red beads Pam gave me," she said.

"Pam's a bit sappy, don't you think?" I asked. Snapping the light off I climbed into my bunk. She didn't answer so I said, "Ginny-winny-ninny-gite."

"Ditto," she answered.

Ditto? Some Twinnish!

Chapter 20

The Johnson House

After Wendy had been to our party and Dad had walked her safely home, her mother actually invited me into their house. It was a bungalow with no veranda. The bungalow was more modern than our old house, but it wasn't as shiny and clean. And it didn't smell as good either. My mother was always polishing and baking so our house always smelled good. Mrs. Johnson just lay around all day smoking Salems and listening to soap-box stories on the radio.

One day Wendy asked her mother if I could stay for supper. "I don't care," her mother answered listlessly from the couch.

So I phoned my mother and got permission.

By six o'clock there was no sign of supper and I was getting hungry. At our house we always sat down promptly at five-thirty, when Dad walked in the door.

"When is your mother going to make supper?" I asked Wendy.

"Oh, she never makes supper. I do."

"You mean you know how to cook?" The most cooking Carrie and I had ever done was toast and tea on Mother's Day.

"Oh, sure. I usually make macaroni and cheese. Do you like it?"

"I've never tasted it, but if there's cheese in it, I'll probably like it."

So Wendy boiled a pot of water and dumped in some dry rattly stuff out of a box. Then, when it was cooked, she drained out the water and stirred in some milk and margarine. Then she ripped open an envelope and sprinkled what looked like orange Jell-O powder over it.

"Here." She handed me a fork. "You can stir."

As I stirred, the powder melted and began to smell like cheese. My stomach rumbled with excitement.

Then Wendy did the strangest thing. Instead of an oilcloth or place-mats, she spread sheets of newspaper on the kitchen table. On top of them she set out three plates, three spoons, three cups with no saucers, and a pint of milk. Then she scooped the macaroni onto our plates.

"Supper's ready, Mom!" she called. Then she said to me, "We might as well start, Connie, because Mom never comes right away."

But this time she did. Carrying a stemmed glass in one hand and a cigarette and ashtray in the other, Mrs. Johnson sat down jerkily at the end of the table. A baby onion swirled around the bottom of her glass. She tipped up the glass and swallowed it. Then she took a puff of her cigarette and before she butted it out she lit another one from its glowing tip.

Wendy had a pot of coffee percolating on the stove.

She even knew how to make coffee! She poured us each a cupful. It was very strong and bitter.

All through the meal Mrs. Johnson didn't say a word. I noticed that two of her fingers were stained the colour of dandelions. There were yellow stains under her nose, too. Between spoonfuls of macaroni she'd take a puff of her cigarette, letting the smoke drift out her nostrils and swirl around her head like a grey halo. Even through the cloud of smoke I could see that she was pretty. She had thick auburn hair — it looked natural, too, not dyed like Lucy's in *I Love Lucy* — and turquoise-blue eyes and dimples in her heart-shaped face. Wendy didn't look the least bit like her mother. She had straight, sandy-brown hair and eyes the mottled blue of blueberries. She must have taken after her father, the same as Carrie and I did, I thought.

I didn't want Mrs. Johnson to catch me staring so I started to read the funnies in the paper under my plate. I moved my plate a bit so I could see the last square.

"So, you're a twin," Mrs. Johnson said suddenly.

"Yes," I said, dropping my spoon on the plate.

"Wendy says you're like two peas in a pod."

"Everybody says that except my Auntie Bea in Canada. She says we're as alike as two brown eggs."

"And you've got brothers, too." As Mrs. Johnson talked smoke drifted out of her mouth and nose simultaneously. She didn't blow it out, it just drifted.

"Yep," I said. "Robbie's fifteen and Jimmy's nine."

"Well, you can tell your mother for me that I said she's a lucky lady." Finishing her coffee in one gulp she picked up her pack of Salems and her overflowing ashtray and went back into the living room and the radio.

Wendy and I did the dishes. That only took a minute because we hadn't used many. She folded the newspaper into a neat package and took it out to the trash can on the back porch. Then we played Chinese checkers on the clean table.

* * *

When I got home I told Mom and Dad all about it. I left out the drink with the onion in it.

"Wendy made supper?" Mom's eyes widened in surprise.

"And you ate off newspapers?" Dad's bottom lip jutted out and his mouth went down at the corners. "And the woman smokes like a chimney?"

Mom gave a sympathetic click of her tongue. "You must ask Wendy over again soon," she said.

While I was talking Carrie hadn't said one word. It wasn't until we were in our bunks that she said, "So you like Wendy a lot, huh?"

"Yes," I said.

"She seems sort of wishy-washy to me," Carrie said.

"Well, she's not. She's very smart. And she's funny sometimes, too." I leaned over the bunk-rail and stared down at my exact likeness. The little gold specks in her eyes were glittering in the light from our seashell nightlight. "Want to hear a joke she told me?"

"No, thanks." Carrie flopped on her side and pulled the cover up to her chin. "I'm sick of her already."

"Well, now you know how I felt about Ruby," I said.

"It's not the same," she said angrily. "Now be quiet. I want to go to sleep. Tomorrow I'm going downtown with Pamela Potter and her mother to buy a girdle and silk stockings."

"A girdle! Silk stockings! I bet Mom won't let you."

"Not for me, silly, for Pam. She's thirteen already."

All of a sudden I felt deflated, like a gas balloon that someone had pricked with a pin. The visit to the Johnsons' didn't seem so interesting anymore. And I had a sinking feeling about Pamela Potter.

Chapter 21

Thick as Jam

Wendy and I became fast friends. Mom said we were as thick as jam. Practically every night we ate at each other's houses. Mom and Dad made a big fuss over Wendy and even Robbie and Jimmy were nice to her. But Carrie sort of ignored her. She wasn't mean or anything. Just indifferent.

One night before an important history test Wendy and me were studying at her kitchen table when her mother, who had not joined us for supper that night, came stumbling into the room.

Tripping over Wendy's book bag, which was leaning against the leg of her chair, Mrs. Johnson yelled a terrible swear word. Then she leaned down with her wet lips not two inches from my face. I pulled back to get away from her smelly breath.

"Are you here again?" she shrieked at me, spraying my face with spit. "Haven't you got a home to go to?"

I was flabbergasted because just the day before she had hugged me and said, "I always wished Wendy had a sister and now I've got my wish."

Wendy gave me a fearful stare.

"I was just leaving." I jumped up and started stuffing my books into my book bag.

"Oh, M–m–mother!" stuttered Wendy, her pale face turning blotchy red. "H–h–how could you say that to C–c–connie!"

Just as suddenly as it had washed over her, the anger drained from Mrs. Johnson's face and she blinked her eyes in surprise. "I was only kidding," she said, playfully tweaking my cheek. "Can't you take a joke, kiddo?" She gave a queer barky laugh. "Where's your funny-bone?"

"Oh, I knew you didn't mean it, Mrs. Johnson. But I have to go home anyway because my mother wants me." It was all I could think of to say.

"Wants you for what?" She slid into a chair and fumbled in her apron pocket for her cigarettes. "She's got lots of kids. She doesn't need you. You stay here."

I didn't know what to do so I glanced at Wendy. Her eyes were swimming with tears.

Luckily the phone rang and Wendy jumped to get it before her mother could.

"Tell whoever it is I'm not home," snapped Mrs. Johnson, lighting her cigarette with shaky yellow fingers. "Tell them nobody's home," she added with another barky laugh.

Wendy held the receiver out toward me. "I–I–It's your m–m–mother," she stuttered.

Mom said it was time for me to come home. "Yes, Mother," I answered obediently. "Right away."

Mrs. Johnson scraped her chair back and went swaying into the living room.

Wendy walked me to the door. "I–I–I'm s–s–sorry, Connie," she whispered.

"It's okay, Wendy," I said. "I'll call for you tomorrow."

Just before the door shut behind me Mrs. Johnson gave a shout from the living room, "You come back, now, you hear me?"

"I will!" I called over my shoulder as I bolted for home.

I wonder who I should tell, I thought. I usually told Carrie everything. But she didn't seem to care about Wendy. Should I tell Mom? No, it would only worry her. Should I tell Dad? I shook my head as I hurried up our front walk. No, he might say I couldn't go there anymore.

As it turned out, I didn't have to tell anybody anything. The very next day Mrs. Johnson was her normal self again. Wendy had calmed down and stopped stuttering, and I began to think I had imagined it all. Maybe Mrs. Johnson *had* been kidding!

Another week went by and everything still seemed fine. Wendy and I wordlessly agreed to forget the whole thing.

"I'm starting to like this individuating," I told Carrie as we flung our bedroom mat over the line and beat it with two sticks. It was a lovely Saturday in May and Mom had the clotheslines full of bedroom mats and blankets, airing them out before storing them in the cedar chest for the summer. "Being friends with Wendy is just like having another sister. Do you feel that way about Pam?"

Carrie was on the other side of the line. She gave the carpet a hard whack with her stick and a cloud of dust puffed right in her face. "Sort of," she gasped.

"What do you mean by sort of?"

"Sort of means sort of!" Dropping the stick on the ground she went in the back door, leaving me to finish the carpet beating.

Right after lunch I called for Wendy.

Mrs. Johnson opened the door. I could tell instantly by the weird look on her face that she had gone peculiar again. "Who are you and what do you want?" she demanded as if I was a stranger.

"It's me, Mrs. Johnson, Connie Taylor. I've come to see Wendy."

"Well, she doesn't need to see you!" she snapped. "So go home and tell your mother she wants you." I got a quick glimpse of Wendy's terrified eyes over her mother's shoulder before Mrs. Johnson shut the door in my face.

This time I knew I had to tell somebody. Wendy's look wasn't just terrified, it was a plea for help. I decided to tell Carrie. I knew that when she sensed how upset I was about Wendy, she'd help, and with two brains to do the thinking, we'd figure out something. But she wasn't home when I got there.

Chapter 22

Betrayed and Deserted

"I wish that twin of yours would come home," Mom said, as the cuckoo clock on the wall over the kitchen table cuckooed six times. "She's been gone all afternoon. Ever since she's been so chummy with that Potter girl she spends more time at their house than ours."

Just then the telephone rang and I jumped to answer it.

It was my sister. "You have to come straight home," I said.

"Let me speak to Mom," she snapped.

I handed the receiver to Mom. "It's Carrie," I said. "Tell her to come straight home."

After a whole lot of hemming and hawing into the phone, Mom said, "Oh, all right, but don't make a habit of it," and hung up.

"Does she want me and Boris Karloff to pick her up?" asked Dad. Pamela Potter lived four blocks away and it was getting dark.

"No. Mrs. Potter has invited her to stay over and I said she could, just this once."

Just this once! And I needed to talk to her so badly. I felt betrayed and deserted. I didn't know what to do. Then I remembered my diary.

Dear Diary: Now I understand how Carrie must have felt about Ruby Butternick. I feel the same way about Wendy Johnson. She's in trouble, and I feel like it's my trouble, too, because we're like sisters. But Pamela Potter! How can Carrie stand her! She's so stuck-up and mean. Just the other day she said to Wendy, "Do you only have one dress?" (Wendy wears the same dress nearly every day.) Poor Wendy blushed and tried to explain that she had lots of dresses but her mother had been too sick lately to iron them. Then the next morning when I called for Wendy she was in tears. She hadn't got her homework done because she'd been up all night ironing. So I let her copy my homework and we were late for school. At recess Carrie asked me how come I was late for school so I told her what Pamela had said. "How can you like somebody that mean?" I asked her. She looked a bit embarrassed, because Carrie is not mean. But just the same, she tried to excuse Pamela. She said, "Oh, she must have been in a bad mood. I'll tell her not to pick on Wendy anymore." To be continued . . .

* * *

I didn't sleep well that night. Luckily on Sunday morning we eat breakfast later than usual, so I could sleep in. I was just coming downstairs when we heard hysterical screams and pounding on our front door. Instantly recognizing Wendy's voice I ran to the door. She almost fell in. She was shivering in her nightgown and bare feet.

Mom's hand flew to her throat. "For mercy's sake,

child, what's the matter?" she cried.

"It's my m–m–mother," stammered Wendy, her face as white as chalk. "She w–w–won't wake up. I y–y–yelled and yelled but she w–w–won't wake up."

Luckily, Dad and Mom were already dressed for church. Dad sprang out of his La-Z-Boy, grabbed Wendy's hand and ran with her out the door. I started to follow them but he called over his shoulder, "You stay there!"

"You kids stay here!" Mom repeated, and ran after them.

Robbie and Jimmy and I stood on the veranda watching helplessly. I wished Carrie was home. I was used to having her beside me in a crisis.

Sunday morning was quiet on Newport Street, except for the twittering of sparrows. Suddenly the silence was shattered by the wail of a siren as an ambulance came speeding up the street and wheeled into the Johnsons' driveway. Two men in white coats leapt out and pulled a stretcher out of the back of the ambulance. Dad held the front door open and they ran in.

The siren had wakened the whole neighbourhood. People stood around in pools on the sidewalks, twittering like sparrows themselves. Then silence fell as the stretcher was carried out the front door, Mrs. Johnson strapped onto it under a grey blanket. Her eyes were shut and her auburn hair was strewn, like red string, on the white pillow.

Mom sent Wendy over to our house, then she and Dad went with Mrs. Johnson in the ambulance.

It was hours before they came home, and we knew by the expressions on their faces that the worst had happened. Gathering us together in the living room, Dad took Wendy on his lap.

"M–m–my mother's d–d–dead, isn't she?" whispered Wendy.

"Yes, my dear." Dad's voice was very tender.

Wendy's mother had swallowed a whole bottle of pills. When they got her to the hospital they pumped her stomach, Dad said, but it was too late. She was dead already.

Chapter 23

Wendy and Carrie and I

The funeral was to be held right in the Johnsons' house, so Mom helped Wendy's aunt, who had come straight down from Port Huron, Michigan, to tidy up and get things ready for the service. The living room was lined with chairs, like a miniature movie theatre. All the neighbours came with flowers.

Mrs. Johnson looked pretty and peaceful in the grey casket. Her auburn hair was curled softly around her heart-shaped face and her cheeks and lips were painted a pearly pink. In her white hands she held a nosegay of rosebuds tied with a white ribbon. Her yellow fingertips were hidden under the green leaves. Through the service Carrie and I sat in the front row on either side of Wendy, holding her hands.

When it was all over Mom and Dad and Wendy's aunt and uncle had a private conference in our kitchen. Then they opened the kitchen door and called us in.

"Wendy . . ." Her aunt brushed the fine brown bangs off Wendy's translucent forehead. "Mr. and Mrs. Taylor have kindly offered to let you stay with them until your uncle and I can decide what's to be done with the house and your mother's things. Would you like that?"

"Yes," Wendy whispered, squeezing my hand.

So Dad put up a cot in our room.

At first only Dad could make Wendy smile. She really liked our dad, which made me think that she'd missed her own Dad more than she had ever let on. Robbie and Jimmy made her welcome, too.

And Carrie was nice to her. We did our homework together and we watched television together and Mom took us all downtown to Crowley's to buy us new white sneakers for summer. So, by the end of the first week Wendy was almost happy.

On Friday night, just for fun, Carrie and I decided to switch bunks to see if we could fool Wendy. So while she was in the bathtub I put on Carrie's red pj's and she put on my green ones and we climbed into each other's bunk.

Wendy came back from the bathroom and slid into the cot. Carrie hung over the rail and said, "Hey, Wendy, what do you want to do tomorrow?"

"Gee, I don't know, Connie. Whatever you and your sister want to do."

"Oh, to heck with her," Carrie said. "Let's do something by ourselves for a change. After all you're my friend, not hers."

"Oh, Connie . . ." Wendy's blueberry eyes switched from the top bunk to the bottom. "I don't want to come between you and your twin sister."

"Shinny-winny-tinny gel jinny-goke?" Carrie asked me.

"Ninny-nonny-ginny-get," I answered.

Translated, Carrie had said, "Shall we let her in on the joke?"

And I had answered, "No, not yet."

Wendy was staring at us as if we were crazy. Mom had come in the middle.

"What language are they talking, Mrs. Taylor?" asked Wendy.

"Dutch." Mom laughed as she kissed us good night, then she said, "What are you two doing in each other's bunks?" She could tell us apart, close up.

"Oh, you bad twins!" laughed Wendy, clapping her hands. "You really had me fooled." It was the first time I'd heard her laugh out loud since the funeral. "Will you teach me your language?"

Carrie and I looked at each other. Then we both shook our heads. "No," we said. "Twinnish is just for twins."

"Oh," said Wendy, and her pale eyes filled with wonder.

Next morning, Wendy said at breakfast, "I wish I could stay here forever."

"Why don't you then?" Jimmy said, glugging down his orange juice. "I like you better than the twins. You're nicer."

"That wouldn't be hard," scoffed Robbie.

"Oh, you shut up," Carrie and I said. And Mom said, "Tut, tut, tut."

I really enjoyed having Wendy in the family, because with her around I didn't mind so much when Carrie played with her other friends. But I could tell when Carrie started getting tired of it. She complained a couple of times about our room being crowded, so Wendy moved her cot over by the wall.

Then the day came when Wendy's aunt and uncle sold the bungalow. We helped Wendy pack her things and she went home with them, to live in Port Huron, Michigan. I missed her terribly, especially after school, when once more I had to walk home alone.

Chapter 24

A Special Lesson

On the Saturday after Wendy left, as we were making up our bunk beds, Carrie surprised me by saying, "Do you want to go to the matinee this afternoon?"

"With who?"

"Me, of course."

"Where's Pamela?" I couldn't keep the sarcasm out of my voice.

"How should I know?" she snapped.

"Did you have a fight?" I asked hopefully.

"No!"

"So why do you want to be twins again?"

"Oh, Connie, don't be so childish." She shook her pillow into a clean pillow-slip and punched it up. "We couldn't stop being twins even if we wanted to. I told Pamela I'd be busy with you for the whole weekend."

"Why?" I asked, suspiciously.

"Because I thought you might be lonely, with wishy-washy Wendy gone."

"She's not wishy-washy!"

"Connie, I was joking! Do you want to go to the show with me or not?"

"Okay," I said. I tried to sound nonchalant but I couldn't keep the happiness out of my voice.

For the whole weekend Carrie and I were together all the time, just like in the old days. We talked Twinnish and laughed all the time and did all the things that only identical twins can do.

On Monday we decided to play one of our old tricks. We dressed exactly alike and did our hair the same. We switched classes and nobody knew the difference.

"After recess" — Mr. Bradley glanced at the pendulum clock above the blackboard. It was twenty-five past two — "the girls are requested to go to Miss Markle's class for a special hygiene lesson."

The boys all started to snicker and we girls all started to blush, even though we didn't know what we were blushing about.

At recess we stood around in bunches talking in whispers.

"What does hygiene mean anyway?" Wilma Fraser asked.

"I think it's all about being healthy," said Merle Shrimp.

"Then why aren't the boys requested?" said Carrie and I.

"It doesn't mean healthy," sniffed Pamela Potter. "It's got something to do with science." Pam was one grade ahead of us so her class wasn't requested to go to Miss Markle's room.

"If it was science the boys would have to go, too," we said.

Then the bell rang.

In Miss Markle's class Carrie and I shared the same seat because there weren't enough desks for everybody. Miss Markle glanced at us, then she looked again. Her eyes narrowed with suspicion. We gave her our widest Doublemint smiles. Mom always said that a smile was disarming, and it must have worked, because she smiled back at us, clapped her hands for attention, and called the class to order.

"Today," she said in her brightest voice, "we're going to discuss a very important subject: personal hygiene."

A wave of whispers rippled over the classroom.

Miss Markle cleared her throat self-consciously. "Now that you are fast becoming young ladies, you may have noticed some bodily changes taking place . . ." She was a bit breathless and her face started to flush as if she was embarrassed. " . . . and when you're very active, when you're skipping rope or playing baseball, you may become quite damp and sticky. This wetness is called perspiration. Now, we all have glands in our armpits that sometimes cause an unpleasant odour. This is sometimes referred to as B.O. It is perfectly natural and nothing to be ashamed of."

We all stared at each other, shame-faced.

"Do I stink?" I whispered to Carrie.

"No. Do I?" She looked really worried.

"No. But maybe we can't tell because we both smell the same."

Every girl in the class was looking doubtfully at the girl beside her. Every girl thought Miss Markle was talking about her!

"Now the way to control this nasty problem," Miss

Markle continued, "is to bathe every day, or at least wash your armpits. Also, you must ask your mothers to buy you an underarm deodorant. Are there any questions?"

Nobody said a word. Then Miss Markle told us what soap to use to ward off this awful problem that boys didn't seem to have. Lifebuoy, she said, was the most effective.

At long last the bell rang and we were dismissed.

On our way home two boys chased after Carrie and me. They seemed to get twice as much fun out of teasing twins.

"Aw, c'mon, tell us what you learned in hygiene class!" begged Dutch Henderson.

"I'll give you an Oh Henry! if you let us in on the secret," wheedled Clarence Webb, waving a candy bar under my nose.

Slapping it away, I grabbed Carrie's hand and we started to run. We ran all the way home and tumbled breathlessly in the kitchen door.

"You have to buy us underarm deodorant, Mom!" we gasped, "and we have to wash every single night with Lifebuoy soap!"

"Deodorant!" Mom rolled her eyes all the way to the ceiling. "A bath every night! For mercy's sake, twice a week is plenty. And children don't need deodorant."

"But Miss Markle says it's our age," I insisted. "The glands under our arms have started to work."

"Well, you can just sponge under there with vinegar and water, the same as I do. It works fine and saves money."

"Then they'll smell like pickles!" snickered Jimmy from the living room.

"He's right for once," we said squinching our noses. "We'll smell like dill pickles."

Mom had to laugh. "More like sweet pickles," she said. Then she added seriously, "We'll take the teacher's advice about the Lifebuoy soap. You can wash with it after you've used the vinegar. That way you'll be doubly protected."

Well, between the vinegar sluices and the smelly orange soap, we were worried sick we'd reek even worse than B.O. But all the mothers must have taken Miss Markle's advice, because every girl in the sixth grade smelled the same. And we noticed something we hadn't noticed before: how awful the boys smelled after baseball practice!

Chapter 25

Pam's Peace Offering

The next weekend was great. There was no sign of Pamela, and Carrie and I were like two peas in a pod again. Then on Sunday afternoon, who should arrive on our front steps, bearing gifts, but Pamela Potter.

She had been away with her parents for the weekend "out of state," she told us with a toss of her blonde curls — as if we'd never been out of Michigan.

"Did you go to Canada?" I asked her.

"No, we went to Buffalo, New York," she said.

"Oh, well," I stuck my nose in the air and tossed my head like a colt, "when we go out of state we go to Toronto, Ontario."

"Ontario — that's a lake, not a country," sneered Pamela.

"You'd better go back to first grade," I sneered back at her. "Because Ontario isn't only a lake, it's a province of Canada."

That took the wind out of her sails for a minute. But then she rallied. "I brought you both a present."

Reaching into a J.C. Penney bag, she handed me a tiny bottle of perfume stamped "sample." Then she gave Carrie a cellophane bag of pink bath salts, tied with a blue ribbon. A sticker on the ribbon said "15 cents."

"Oh, thank you, Pam!" Carrie cooed, sniffing the bag. "It smells lovely." I shot her a disdainful look for being so easily pleased.

"It's essence of gardenias," bragged Pamela.

"Why are you giving us this stuff?" I asked suspiciously.

"Well, you know . . ." Pamela fluttered her curly eyelashes. "I thought it might help with your problem."

"What problem?" we demanded.

"Umm, well, you know . . . what you found out in hygiene class."

All of a sudden I saw red. "Well you'd better keep this stinky old 'sample' for yourself because you're the one with the problem." I threw the dinky bottle back into her bag and yelled, "Thanks for nothing!" and stomped into the house.

I was hoping Carrie would do the same with her bath salts, but she didn't. Instead she used them that night in the bathtub and soaked in there for hours until Dad pounded on the door and made her come out.

Then she came wafting into our room in a damp, perfumy cloud. "Pee-yew!" I gagged and dove under the blanket.

Mom popped her head in our door and gasped for air. "For mercy's sake!" she cried, "What stinks in here?"

"It's Pamela Potter's bath salts, Mom," I said from my hiding place. "Make Carrie wash it off with Lifebuoy before I smother under here."

Mom just laughed and I heard her kiss Carrie good night, then she leaned over the rail and kissed me through the sheet.

* * *

Halfway through the night the light suddenly switched on and there was Carrie jumping all over the room, like a flea, scratching herself. A red rash had broken out all over her body.

Mom got up and made her take a baking-soda bath. The next day she threw the remains of the bath salts into the trash can.

"Please don't tell Pamela, Connie," begged Carrie, on the way to school. She was still scratching through her sweater.

Oh, boy, I thought, what a swell chance to get even. "Well, are you going to stay friends with her? After she practically told us we stink?" I demanded.

"Oh, Connie. It's not her fault that the bath salts gave me a rash. And besides, I'm sure she meant it as a peace offering. She was kind of mad, that weekend I told her I couldn't see her. That stuff about our 'problem' was just a joke."

"A joke! Carrie Taylor, how can my twin be so dumb? Pamela Potter is really mean. Don't you remember how she treated Wendy? And she spread that rumour all over the school that the Flints had fleas."

"Oh, that's just her funny sense of humour, Connie. She doesn't mean anything."

Suddenly I read Carrie's mind. "Do you know what I think?" She didn't answer so I told her what I thought. "I think you're afraid of Pamela Potter. You'd rather have her for a friend than an enemy."

Carrie stopped short and shot me a cold look, one I'd never seen on her face before. "Well, you know what I think? I think you're jealous because you haven't got a best friend now that Wendy's gone. You want me all to yourself. Well, forget it!"

She stomped away and left me fuming on the sidewalk.

But she had read my mind. I did want her all to myself. I wanted everything to be like it used to be, her and me, mirror images, talking Twinnish in our own little world.

After school I hurried home, not wanting to see Carrie leave with Pamela. Throwing my book bag in the door I slouched onto a kitchen chair. I heard my mother in the cellar unloading the washing machine. Then the lid clacked shut and she came up the stairs hefting the heavy clothes basket.

Setting the basket on the top step she wiped a damp wavy strand of hair out of her eyes. "What are you moping about, Connie?" she asked.

"I'm not moping. I'm mad," I grumbled. "I'm beginning to wish I wasn't born a twin after all."

"Oh, you don't mean that," she said. Then she heaved the basket up and headed for the back door. "Come and help me peg out the wash and tell me what's bothering you."

Through the flapping sheets and towels, I confessed to Mom how jealous I was of Pamela Potter. How I wanted Carrie to need only me for a friend. "I don't need anybody else, so why should she, Mom? She didn't used to. We always thought we were lucky because we were born best friends. But now she wants to be different. And

I don't understand. Why would Carrie change, Mom?"

Mom looked at me over the grey work-shirt she was pinning on the line by the tails. "I'm not sure what's going on in her mind, Connie," she said through a clothespeg pursed between her lips. "But I think you and Carrie should try to settle it yourselves. I can't take sides, you know."

We finished pegging out the wash and went inside.

"I guess I'll talk to her myself," I said.

"That's a good idea," Mom agreed, stroking my hair.

Just then Robbie came in from high school and plunked a big pile of books, strapped together with his belt, on the table. "I've got enough homework to choke a horse," he complained. Then he looked at me. "Hey, how come you're home? I just saw Carrie with that gorgeous Potter girl and she flirted with me like crazy. I might ask her out."

"If you do I'll tell Betty Pool," I threatened.

"Go ahead," Robbie laughed, feeling his chin for whiskers. "Pamela Potter is way cuter than Betty Pool anyway. Yeah, I think I'll ask her to the show."

"Well you can just think again," I snapped. "'Cause Pamela Potter is not allowed to date yet. So there!"

Chapter 26

Oh, No!

Carrie stayed so late at Pamela's house that night that Mom had to send Robbie over to get her. And when she came in the door I yelled, "Oh, no! What have you done?"

Instead of shoulder-length wavy brown hair like mine, her whole head was covered in a million corkscrew curls.

"You look like a French poodle," laughed Jimmy.

"You shut up, Jimmy." Carrie pushed past him to the mirror. "Mrs. Potter gave Pam and me a Toni Home Permanent, Mom. Do you like it?"

"Well, you should have asked my permission first," Mom said, pulling the tight little curls one by one and letting them spring back. "I don't know what your father's going to say. He's so proud of his twins' naturally wavy hair."

"But, Mom," Carrie argued, "Tonis are all the rage now. Connie can get one, too, if she likes."

"Oh, sure," I said disgustedly. "And then everybody

will say, 'Which twin has the Toni? Which twin has the Toni?' just like on television."

"I think she looks cute," Robbie casually remarked.

Carrie and I both gaped at him. He hardly ever noticed how we looked.

Just then we heard Boris Karloff choke to a stop out the front.

"Uh-oh!" Jimmy said. "Dad's home."

Dad came in the front door whistling some tune from the past. When he saw Carrie he stopped short, his mouth still shaped like an O. "What in blazes have you done to yourself?" he demanded.

"It's just a Toni Home Permanent, Dad," Carrie said.

"Well, go upstairs and wash it out," he ordered. "I like your hair natural, like your sister's."

"It won't wash out," Mom explained to him. "It's a permanent wave. It will have to grow out."

"Well, I've got an idea how to make it grow out fast," Dad said. "Tomorrow, young lady, you can come with me to the barbershop and get it cut into a boyish bob. How would that suit you?"

"Oh, no!" I cried. "Then we'll be even more different."

"Well, I just got another idea." Dad seemed to be full of ideas. "You can come, too, Connie and you can both get boyish bobs. Then you'll be identical again and it'll be nice and cool for summer. That's what's known as killing two birds with one stone."

"Well, this is what's known as putting your foot down." Mom actually stamped her foot on the floor. "No boyish bobs for my girls. There are two boys in this family already and that's enough."

Dad threw up his hands and went to the sink to wash.

I went into the living room to watch T.V. with Jimmy, and Carrie slunk upstairs, not sure whether she'd won or lost.

The following week at school, sure enough, the kids all danced around us teasing, "Which twin has the Toni? Which twin has the Toni?" They kept it up day after day until Carrie ran home in tears.

"Don't cry." Mom twisted a curl around her finger. "You know," she said. "I think Robbie's right. You do look cute. The short hair suits you. It makes your face appear rounder." Taking both our chins in her cupped hands she stared first at Carrie, then at me. "Yes, the longer hair stretches out your face, Connie. What do you say I give you a Toni Home Permanent, too?"

To my surprise I said, "Okay."

So that very night Mom permed my hair. And the next day, both twins had the Toni.

Miss Markle was on yard duty in the schoolyard and as soon she spotted me she said, "You might have fooled me once, Caroline Taylor. But not twice. I know you're not Conroy."

I laughed and said, "Yes, I am, Miss Markle. I am Conroy." I could hardly believe that name had come out of my mouth. I'd never called myself Conroy before. It didn't sound so bad after all. "Last night my mother gave me a Toni, too, so now Carrie and I are identical again. But I can prove I'm Conroy." Lifting the curls up on the right side of my head I showed her my bent ear. "One of Carrie's ears is bent, too, but it's her left ear. That's how our parents tell us apart."

Miss Markle looked, then smiled at me warmly. "I

appreciate your telling me that, Conroy. Thank you."

"You're welcome." I smiled back. "But don't tell the other kids, please Miss Markle, because they'll never stop teasing us if they find out."

"Don't worry," she said, locking her lips with an imaginary key. "Your secret's safe with me."

Then she rang the bell and I ran to my line and marched in behind my sister.

Chapter 27

Freda Friday

If we thought it was hard to dry our hair before, it was worse with our Tonis. If we got caught in the rain, the curls got so frizzy we couldn't get a comb through them. So, one day when it was pouring rain Carrie and I were standing in the school doorway waiting for it to let up. Someone came out behind us and said, "Hey, Carrie, want to share my bumbershoot?"

It was Freda Friday. She was in Carrie's class, but I'd heard all about her. She was new to our school. She was big and tall and tough. She had short black hair, beady black eyes like a bird's, and she played baseball like a boy. And she was smart, too — she had skipped a grade into Mr. Bradley's class.

Freda had snapped open a big red umbrella. Carrie shifted her books to her other arm. "Uh, okay," she said. Before I could say anything, Freda strode off with my twin sister under her bumbershoot.

I ran home in the rain mad as hops. Even though I took a shortcut, when I got home my Toni was plastered to my head in a million kiss-curls.

I let the kitchen door slam shut and Mom cried, "Oh, no!" Then she flung open the oven door. Her angel-food cake had collapsed like a flat tire.

"Now see what you made me do, Carrie Taylor!" She still got us mixed up sometimes when she was mad or excited. Lifting the cake pan out of the oven with a tea towel, she put it on the counter. "What am I going to do? This cake was for the church bake sale. I haven't got time to make another one."

Then she did a double-take. "Oh, it's you, Connie. Why do you try to fool me like that? Where's your sister?"

I didn't know which question to answer first so I said, "I'm sorry, Mom."

"Here, dry your head before you catch your death." She threw me a towel from the spoke above the stove. "Then you can run down to Fanny's Bakery for me and get another angel food." She poked a straw into the side of the cake and it collapsed again with a little puff of steam. "We'll have this for supper and I'll frost the store-bought cake and hope nobody is the wiser."

I rubbed my head dry with the towel, then ran upstairs to change my dress and comb my frizzy hair.

Mom gave me a dollar bill. "Now don't lose it, and be sure to tell Mildred — she's the lady with the blue hair — that the cake is for Mrs. Taylor. She always makes sure I get today's goods."

The rain had stopped, and a lovely rainbow arced over the houses on the other side of Newport Street.

I skipped down to Jefferson, turned the corner, and ran smack into Carrie and Freda Friday.

"Oh, hi, Connie," my twin sister said as if everything was hunky-dory.

"You're going to get it," I said, frowning at her. "Mom asked me where you were and I said I didn't know."

"Oh, phooey!" she tossed her frizzy curls. "It's only early."

Freda was staring at me as if she was seeing things, her black bird's eyes darting back and forth between me and Carrie. "How come you two look exactly alike?" she asked suspiciously, as if we were playing tricks.

Hadn't my sister told Freda she was a twin? "You're probably seeing double," I said, smart-alecky.

"You must be twins," Freda said.

"No kidding." I started walking backward towards the bakery. "I gotta get a cake for Mom," I said. "Hers fell in."

"Do you want to come home and meet my mother?" Carrie asked Freda.

At the bakery door I said, "You'd better not. Mom's in a cranky mood."

"Oh, she won't mind. Our Mom is nice," she told Freda. So I yelled, "Well, then wait for me!" I dashed into the bakery, ordered the cake from blue-haired Mildred, and caught up to them, swinging the box by the string.

We met Robbie in front of our house. "Whatcha got there, Twinny?" he asked me, licking his lips like a dog.

"It's not for us," I said. "It's for the church."

Then Carrie said, "Robbie, this is my new friend, Freda Friday. Freda, this is my brother, Robbie."

"Hi!" Robbie said as he leapt up the steps in a single bound.

"He's cute!" squawked Freda, loud enough for him to hear.

Oh, no, not another boy-crazy, I thought.

Carrie introduced Freda to Mom. Mom just nodded because she was too busy to be friendly. So Carrie got Fig Newtons from the pantry and milk from the Frigidaire and two plastic tumblers from the cupboard.

Mom frosted both cakes at once and as soon as she was finished she gave Jimmy the icing bowl to lick. "Your friend better go home now, Carrie," Mom said rather shortly. "It's nearly suppertime and it's your turn to set the table."

Embarrassed, Carrie walked Freda out onto the veranda and I heard her say through the screen door, "Will I see you tomorrow, Freda?"

"Okay," Freda said. "But you'd better come home to my house. My mother will probably invite you to supper."

"Thanks," Carrie said, then she went back into the kitchen and began banging the plates on the table.

* * *

Sure enough, the very next day Carrie went home with Freda. After supper I went out to the veranda. I was swinging on the glider and feeling sorry for myself when Pamela Potter came riding up our street on her brand new two-wheeler. When she saw me she stopped in front of our house.

I could tell by the puzzled look on her face that she wasn't sure which twin I was, so I said, hoping to get rid of her, "Carrie's not home. She's at Freda Friday's"

"Oh." Pam pulled a face. "Well, is it okay if I come up?"

"I guess." I was bored anyway and Pam was better than nobody.

Dropping her bike sideways on our lawn, she

bounded up the veranda steps. The glider squawked as she plunked down beside me. She was too close for comfort so I shoved over.

"I don't know how Carrie can stand that Froggy Freda," Pam said, tossing her blonde head contemptuously.

"Froggy Freda!" A screech of laughter burst out of me at that horrible nickname. "I never heard her called that before."

"Well, haven't you noticed?" snickered Pam, cozying up to me. "Her hands are all warty, like a frog. So I call her Froggy Freda."

I laughed again, which was a mistake, because that was all the encouragement she needed. "She's so ugly and mean even the boys are afraid of her," she blabbered. "So why would Carrie like her? Besides, my mother says she's not from a very nice family. They live over a store on Jefferson Street and Mom says all those apartments have mice and bugs and . . ."

On and on she went. After a while I thought, good grief, I'd rather be bored. Then Mom poked her head out the door, coming to my rescue. "Connie, haven't you got homework?"

"Yes, Mom," I said, and went right in.

I was at the kitchen table just finishing up when Carrie came home. "Hey, Carrie," I said. "Guess who came over to keep me company?"

"Who?" She was instantly suspicious.

"Pamela Potter, that's who. We had a swell time." Crossing my fingers under the table I added, "I think I like her after all."

"Can't you even make your own friends?" Carrie

121

snapped. "Do you have to horn in on mine?"

"Well, it's a free country!" I snapped back as she ran upstairs.

That night we had a big fight in the bathroom.

"I got this awful perm just for you," I yelled, yanking the hairbrush through my tangled curls.

"Well, who asked you to? I got the perm on purpose to individuate."

Hearing that stupid word again made me so mad that I reached out and pulled her darn hair. Then she grabbed a fistful of mine and we tumbled around on the bathroom floor, kicking and screaming.

"You're just jealous of my new friend!" she screeched.

"Who would be jealous of 'Froggy Freda'?" I screeched back.

Suddenly we heard Dad's footfalls pounding up the stairs.

Jumping up we turned on the taps in the bathtub but he banged on the door so loud we had to open it.

"What's going on in here?" he demanded.

"She started it," Carrie said. "She pulled my hair."

"Why did you pull your sister's hair?"

"Because . . ." I couldn't think of a good reason.

"And she called my new friend 'Froggy Freda'!" She had never snitched on me before.

Dad turned on me angrily, twisting the newspaper into a tight roll between his fists. "Why would you say such a nasty thing, Connie?" he demanded.

"Because Freda's got warts all over her hands. I didn't make it up. Pamela Potter calls her that all the time."

But blaming somebody else didn't work with our dad. He swatted me with the twisted newspaper all the way into my bed. I scrambled up the ladder and tunneled down under the covers and jammed my face into the pillow.

After he'd gone I kept my face hidden in my pillow to muffle the sobs. It wasn't the swatting I was crying about — it hadn't hurt that much — but the fact that my twin sister was busy individuating again.

Chapter 28

Welcome Advice

The phone was ringing as I walked in the kitchen door, so I answered it.

"Hello."

It was Aunt Sylvia. "Is that Connie or Carrie?" she asked. Everybody always said we sounded as if we were mimicking each other on the telephone. "It's me, Connie, Aunt Sylvia."

"How are you, Connie?"

"Okay, I guess."

"Well, dear, could you possibly come over and watch Ronnie for an hour or so? I have to go to the drugstore and Marilyn's not home." Marilyn was Aunt Sylvia's beautiful teenage daughter. Ronnie was Marilyn's little brother, just the age of our Jimmy but forever a baby in his mind. Aunt Sylvia never left him alone.

"Sure, Aunt Sylvia." I was glad to have something to do. "I'll be right over."

Ronnie was sitting in his special chair when I got there. Uncle Phil had fixed it up with a brace shaped like a horse collar to hold his head up, and a wooden tray in front to keep him from sliding out. Ronnie had a huge head, nearly as big as a beach ball, and round Dresden-china-blue eyes and fluffy white hair. He was easy to amuse, being so simple.

When Aunt Sylvia got back she put him to bed. Uncle Phil had made a huge crib for Ronnie and it took all of Aunt Sylvia's strength to heft him over the side. Then she leaned over the rail and blew a furrow through his soft, downy white hair. The wind in his hair made Ronnie coo like a dove. Then he shut his big eyes and fell instantly asleep.

Back in the kitchen Aunt Sylvia went to the Kelvinator and got out a bottle of Pepsi Cola. "Is something troubling you, Connie?" she asked. "You're not your usual smiley self. And where's your other half today?"

"She's the trouble," I said.

"Do you want to tell me about it?"

The concern in her voice made me bubble up and cry. Aunt Sylvia was easy to talk to so I told her all about Carrie always making new friends for individuating.

"So you think your twin wants to get unhitched?" Aunt Sylvia poured the Pepsi into two glasses and opened up a fresh package of Oreos.

"She says not, but that's what it feels like to me," I complained, blowing my nose on the Kleenex she handed me. Then I broke an Oreo in half and scraped the icing off with my two front teeth.

"Hmm." She stirred the fizz out of her soda with a swizzle stick. "That reminds me of something. I minded Carrie one day when the two of you were three or four years old; your mother had taken you someplace else . . .

I don't remember where . . . I should, since it was so seldom that she took one without the other. Well, little Carrie was looking at herself in my hand-mirror and I'll never forget what she said. 'Aunt Silby' — that's what you twins used to call me when you were little — 'Aunt Silby,' she said, gazing into the mirror, 'I don't know who I are!' Those were her very words: 'I don't know who I are.'"

"Oh, Aunt Sylvia," I gasped. "I know exactly what she meant. I get that same feeling sometimes when I look in the mirror."

"Well, dear . . ." Aunt Sylvia reached out and squeezed my hand. "I think if you just leave her alone, let her go her own way and you go yours, then, when she's found herself, she'll come back to you. My mother used to say, 'If you keep a bird in a cage and it escapes, you'll never see it again. But if you let it fly free, it will always come back to you.'"

She opened her change purse and pressed a quarter into my hand. I shook my head no, but Aunt Sylvia insisted. "Did what I said make any sense, Connie?" she asked, closing my fist around the quarter.

"Oh, yes!" I said. "Thanks a lot, Aunt Silby!"

I walked home slowly, thinking all the way about Aunt Sylvia's mother's story about the caged bird. It reminded me of a pet bird we used to have, named Petey. When he managed to escape his cage he was almost impossible to catch. But, if we just let him fly free, the next thing we knew he'd land right on our shoulders.

Chapter 29

Girl Scouts

I decided to take Aunt Sylvia's advice and go my own way. "You know what, Mom," I said. "I think I'm going to join the Girl Scouts." I had seen Mary-Ann Hubbard and Ollie Swinson in their scout uniforms and they looked really smart. And I liked uniforms. Especially policemen's.

"Oh, that sounds like a good idea, Connie. You'll make new friends there. After all, what do girls who don't have a twin do? I think you'll like it, Connie — and I can just picture you in a Girl-Scout uniform. You'll be cute as a buttercup."

"Cute as a buttercup. I never heard you say that before, Mom," I laughed.

"Oh, that's an old saying I just made up," she quipped.

So I went right across the street and called for Mary-Ann Hubbard. "What do I have to do to join the Girl Scouts?" I asked her.

"Well, there's a meeting in the church basement

tonight at seven o'clock," Mary-Ann said. "You can come with me and Ollie Swinson and find out."

So I went and the first thing I learned was that you never just say Girl Scouts, you have to say "Girl Scouts of America."

Then our leader, a tall lady in a beige uniform with bright red lips and a golden mustache, taught us newcomers (there were three of us) how to salute the flag. Then she gave us a list of things we needed: a uniform and tools and a nickel for dues.

After that we all sat down on benches around a long wooden table — like the picnic table in High Park in Toronto — and the leader gave us each a ball of many-coloured wool and a wooden spool with no thread on it. The spool had four little nails hammered into it around the hole in the centre.

"What are these for?" I asked Ollie Swinson, who was sitting next to me.

"Cork-work. We're making pot-holders for our mothers' birthdays." Ollie answered in a whisper — so I guessed you weren't supposed to talk out loud. Maybe because we were in the church basement.

"My mother's birthday is the same day as ours — uh — mine," I whispered back. "And it's gone past already."

"Well, make it for Christmas then. Here, I'll get you started."

Taking my spool she twisted a strand of wool around each nail and pulled about six inches through the hole. Then she showed me how to loop the strands over the nails and pull it through. I looped and pulled and looped and pulled for about an hour and gradually a knitted rope appeared through the hole.

Just before the meeting was over a pie tin was passed around and everybody dropped their nickels in, ping, ping, ping. I promised the leader I'd bring my nickel next week. We all stood up and put our right hands over our hearts and sang "God Bless America." Then Mary-Ann and Ollie walked me home.

"Did you like Girl Scouts of America?" asked Mary-Ann.

"It was okay," I said. Then I ran up our front steps.

Dad peered over his glasses through the open French doors. "Where have you been, Connie?" he asked.

"Girl Scouts," I said.

"What did you do there?"

"Cork-work."

He went back to his newspaper and I went upstairs.

I knew, as I stuffed the cork-work in the back of my drawer behind my underwear, that I'd never finish the pot-holder. I didn't like cork-work and I'd found something out about myself that I didn't know before: I wasn't a joiner. I didn't want to be a Girl Scout.

"What are you hiding, Connie?" Carrie was sitting at our desk studying.

"Nothing," I said. I put on my pj's and climbed up the ladder into my bunk and got my diary from under my pillow.

June 12, 1954.
Dear Diary: I have decided to be a loner. Twins,
especially identical twins, are not supposed to be loners, but
when your mirror twin decides to individuate and makes
new best friends all the time then you either have to do the
same or be a loner. To be continued . . .

Chapter 30

Carrie Takes a Stand

It was recess, the last day of school, and I was sitting by myself on a smooth, sun-warmed rock at the end of the schoolyard. I was daydreaming about what we might do on our summer holidays. I had heard Dad talking to Mom about going to Toronto again and Mom had said maybe we should do something different for a change, like rent a camper on Lake St. Clair or take a trip to Niagara Falls.

The rock I was sitting on was hidden from the playground by spirea bushes. There was a cherry tree outside the school fence and a robin was gathering bits of string and fluff for her nest. I was being very quiet so as not to scare her when I heard voices on the other side of the bushes.

"You're sooo different from your sister." I recognized Freda Friday's smart-alecky way of talking. "She's sooo stuck up."

I held my breath, cupped my ear and listened harder.

"No, she's not. Connie's not stuck up at all. And we're

not different — we're exactly the same."

"Oh, you look the same, all right, but that's not what I mean. You don't act the same. You're friendly and nice and she's stand-offish."

The next words I heard scared the robin right out of the tree and made me gasp. "You shut up, Freda Friday!" screamed my sister.

Then I heard Freda say in a low, mean voice, "I'll let you off this time, Carrie Taylor, 'cause I know you didn't mean it. Isn't that right, Carrie? You didn't mean to tell me to shut up, did you?"

"Nooo," said Carrie, sounding scared.

"Then say you're sorry."

"I'm sorry." Carrie's voice quavered.

"All right, then." The bell rang and they started walking away. "But watch your mouth after this." Then their voices got lost in the hubbub of the schoolyard.

I wasn't mad at Carrie for being scared of Freda. Freda was a bully and nearly all the kids were afraid of her. Even the boys. All that mattered to me was that my twin had said, "We're not different, we're exactly the same."

At last school let out for the summer, and everyone raced home to get started on vacation. Carrie came in soon after me. She didn't say anything about her fight with Freda Friday, but that night we talked like old times in our bunks that night and Dad had to holler up a warning before we would settle down.

The next morning, Carrie said, "What are you going to wear today, Connie?"

"My new shorts outfit," I said. Mom had ordered them out of Sears-Roebuck as a reward for passing with honours.

"Okay. I'll wear mine too."

We combed our hair the same way and parted it down the middle and clipped it on the sides with matching barrettes.

When we came down to breakfast Mom smiled delightedly and clapped her hands. "Oh, now that's more like it. My twinny-twin-twins," she cried, patting our identical heads.

Jimmy stuck his finger down his throat and gagged, "Yuck!"

"I second it — yuck!!" agreed Robbie. Jumping up from the table, he kissed Mom on the cheek and headed for the kitchen door. "I don't want to be late on my first day," he said.

Robbie had got himself a job in the back of Blood's Butcher Shop on Jefferson Street, mincing hamburger and stuffing sausages.

"Don't forget to bring home a pound of bangers for supper!" Mom called after him.

Carrie and I were still too young to get a real summer job but Aunt Sylvia had hired us to amuse Ronnie once a week while she was at her bridge club and she said she would pay us each a quarter. So on the first day of summer holidays we phoned to see when she wanted us and she said to come right over. It wasn't bridge day, she said, but she'd go shopping instead.

On our way over who should we meet but Pamela Potter. Pamela hadn't spoken to Carrie since Carrie had become friends with Freda Friday, and she'd completely ignored me since that day on our veranda. But today she walked right up to us with a big phoney smile on her face. "Hi!" she said, tossing her long blonde hair over one shoulder. "Are you two going anywhere for your holidays?"

"Maybe to Niagara Falls," we said.

"Oh, I've been there dozens of times," boasted Pam.

"On the Canadian side?" I asked.

"Oh, no, we never cross the border. My Dad says it's too uncivilized up there."

"Gee, I can hardly wait to tell that to my cousin, Bart," I said sarcastically. "He's coming over soon. Maybe he'll bring his pet polar bear — if they can fit him into the car."

Pam's eyes stretched so big you could see all the whites around the chocolate-coloured irises. "Has he really got a pet polar bear?" she cried.

"Oh, don't listen to her." Carrie gave me a poke. "She's just being silly."

Then I said, "C'mon, Carrie. We gotta go or we'll be late for our job." And Carrie called over her shoulder, "Be seeing you, Pam."

"Do you still like her?" I asked Carrie as we turned up Aunt Sylvia's street.

Carrie's arched golden-brown eyebrows pulled together in a frown. "I like her in a way — she's not a bully like Freda. But I don't really want to individuate with her anymore."

"That's a relief," I said.

Ronnie was so happy to see us that he smiled and slobbered and cooed like a dove all afternoon. We did such a good job of minding him that Uncle Phil, who got home before Aunt Sylvia, gave us each a half-dollar (or four bits as he called it) instead of a quarter.

On the second day of summer holidays Pamela

phoned while we were having lunch. Mom handed Carrie the bell-shaped receiver. Carrie listened, smiling and nodding her head. "Okay, if Connie can come too." I shook my head, no, but Carrie ignored me. Then she said, "See you later," and hung up.

"Come where?" I asked.

"Pam says there's a travelling fair in the vacant lot on Blantyre Street where the old fire hall used to be and she wants us to go with her."

Then Mom said, "You're not going anywhere until you've cleaned your room."

"I'll bet we're the only kids who have to do work on summer holidays," we complained.

"I'll bet," Mom agreed.

We raced upstairs and went through our room like a cyclone. Then Mom came up, rolled her eyes, and said she guessed it would have to do.

Chapter 31

The Ferris Wheel

Carrie lectured me all the way down Newport Street. "Now, Connie," she said, wagging her finger in my face. "Let's try to share our friends instead of being jealous all the time. Okay?"

"I guess."

"Try to be nice to Pam. Then she'll be nice to you."

"Huh!" I said. "Okay, but it won't be easy."

Pam met us at the corner and we walked along Jefferson together. When we heard the screams from the amusements we broke into a run.

"The Ferris wheel is our favourite ride. What's yours?" we hollered over the noise.

"I'm not going on the rides," Pam yelled back.

"Why not?" we asked breathlessly.

"Because they're just for kids. Let's go to the midway and play the games of chance."

"But we like the rides," we said.

"The games are more fun," Pam insisted. "And there'll be boys there."

"What boys?" we asked.

"Del Paige for one. He's in high school now. Remember him? He's got a summer job on the Dart Game."

"What's the Dart Game?" we asked.

"You throw darts at balloons and win a prize. I'll bet he'll give me the biggest prize," she said, batting her eyelashes.

"I'll bet," we said.

Suddenly Pam put her hands on her hips and glared at us. "Why do you two do that?" she demanded.

"Do what?" we asked.

"That. What you just did. Talk together all the time. You sound like a couple of stupid parrots."

"So! At least we're not stupid boy-crazies." I spoke by myself that time.

Pam turned on her heel and flounced off toward the midway.

"Oh, Connie." Carrie started after Pam, so I grabbed her by the hand and pulled her toward the ticket wicket.

We went on five rides, then we bought pink cotton candy on paper cones. I ripped a strip off and stuffed it into my mouth as I stared up at the Ferris wheel. We had saved our favourite ride for last.

Just then Pam appeared beside us. I couldn't help but notice she was empty-handed.

"You coming on?" we asked.

"NO!" she snapped.

"Okay. You can hold our cones," we said, and before she could object we thrust them into her hands and got on the Ferris wheel.

Swooping by in breathtaking circles, we waved and

screamed at Pam, who couldn't wave back because her hands were full.

On the third revolution of the giant wheel, just as we reached the top, it jolted to a stop. From there we had a panoramic view of the whole city of Detroit. But try as we might we couldn't pick out our house on Newport Street.

After a while we realized that we had been up there for a long time. So we leaned over the safety bar, tipping our seat precariously, to see what was going on down below. The people on the ground looked like tiny puppets staring up at us. And little men were scurrying, like ants, in all directions.

"Uh-oh," I said. "I think we're stuck up here."

We were marooned under the cloudless sky for an hour and we started to burn in the afternoon sun. Sweat soaked our hair and trickled down our necks and our Toni home permanents began to look like Kurly-Kate pot-cleaners.

Suddenly our boiling hot seat jerked into motion, curved over the top, and slowly began to descend. We staggered off the Ferris wheel on wobbly rubber legs.

Pam was furious. She'd thrown our cotton candy cones away but not before melting pink sugar had run in rivers down her arms and dripped off her elbows.

Pam didn't speak to us all the way home. She just kept repeating, "Eww! Eww! Eww!" as she spit on her sticky elbows and scrubbed them with her hanky. At the corner of her street she turned on us and screeched, "I hate you both, you stupid parrots!" Then she flounced off home.

"Good riddance to bad rubbish!" I yelled after her.

"Well, now you did it," snapped Carrie.

"Did what?"

"You insulted Pam again and now she's mad and probably won't speak to me all the rest of the summer."

"Well, do you really care? Who wants to be friends with a dumbbell who thinks Canadians have polar bears for pets?"

Carrie had to laugh, then she started to run, yelling over her shoulder, "Last one home's a stupid parrot!"

I let her win and we got home just in time to see "Queen for a Day" on television.

"Did you have fun at the fair?" Mom asked. She was feather-dusting the green panther on top of the Motorola with her usual distaste.

We looked at each other and read each other's minds. If we told her we had got stuck for an hour on top of the Ferris wheel she'd probably never let us go to a fair again as long as we lived. So we said, "Yes, Mom, we had lots of fun."

"Then run upstairs and jump into the bath." Feather-dusting the magazine rack beside the sofa, she looked at us more closely. "What happened to your noses?" she asked. Crossing our eyes, we looked down our noses. They were as red as Rudolph's. "How did you get such a sunburn?"

"There's no shade in the fairgrounds." We spoke in unison as if we had rehearsed it. "Why do we have to have a bath before supper?"

"Because you smell to high heaven." Mom's nose had got extra sensitive to B.O. ever since that hygiene lesson. "There's a bottle of vinegar-and-water on the windowsill. Give yourselves a good sluice under your arms then lather up with the Lifebuoy."

Chapter 32

Canadian Visitors

Our summer holidays were halfway over before anything really interesting happened.

"They'll be here any minute," Mom said, glancing at the cuckoo clock. "So why don't you two go out and wait on the veranda?"

We were all dressed up in our birthday frocks (Mom's English word for dresses) and Aunt Sylvia, who used to be a hairdresser, had trimmed our Tonis into a lovely, fluffy, feather cut. We were swinging on the glider when who should walk by our house, arm in arm, but Pamela Potter and Kitty Foxcroft.

Pam pointed at us without turning her head. "Oh, lookie!" she squealed. "It's the Bobbsey twins!"

"Their name isn't 'Bobbsey'," corrected Kitty as they went prancing by. "It's Taylor." Pam's sarcasm had gone right over her head, proving how dumb she was.

I was just about to yell after them that I'd rather be a Bobbsey than a dumbbell when Uncle Dave and Auntie Rose drove up in their rusty old Durante.

We leaped down the veranda steps and smothered Auntie Rose in hugs the minute she stepped out of the car.

"Oh, aren't you beautiful," she cried, patting our fluffy brown heads.

Uncle Dave laughed and coughed and lit another cigarette. "I'd better get my peepers tested," he said, fanning the smoke out of his eyes. "I'm starting to see double."

Bart jumped out of the back seat and hollered, "Where's Robbie?" Jimmy came flying down the steps and said, "He's at work." Then Mom and Dad came out the front door and we had a joyous reunion on the veranda.

"I see you're still driving that old rust-bucket," was the first thing Dad said to his brother. Mom just rolled her eyes and pulled Auntie Rose into the house.

Bart sat between us twins on the glider and asked, "What's new?" So we told him about our adventure on the Ferris wheel.

"Does Mom know?" piped up Jimmy.

We were so busy looking at Bart — he was so cute we wished he wasn't our cousin — that we forgot Jimmy was sitting there on the top step with his big ears. "No, and if you tell her you'll be sorry," we threatened.

"Okay, I won't tell," Jimmy said agreeably. "Where's Norman, Bart?"

"He went to Rice Lake with his new girlfriend," replied Bart.

I was just about to ask if she was pretty, when Pam and Kitty came walking back up the street. The minute they spied Bart they sashayed, uninvited, right up our front walk. "Hi, Carrie! Hi, Connie!" sang Pam in a honey-sweet voice.

Carrie said, "Hi," but I didn't.

"Aren't you going to introduce us?" asked Pamela, tossing her shiny blonde hair over her shoulder and batting her paint-brushy eyelashes.

"This here's our cousin, Bart, from Canada," Jimmy said.

"Yeah," I said. "The one with the pet polar bear."

"I didn't see no polar bear," Jimmy said.

I couldn't believe that our own brother was a dumb as those two. But of course he had an excuse — he was only ten years old.

"That's because I just got him last Christmas," said Bart, catching on right away.

"Have you got pictures of him?" asked Kitty. She was serious!

Then Pam said, "Can we come up, Carrie?" She was looking straight at me so I knew she had us mixed up. I was just about to say, "No you can't," when Dad appeared at the screen door and saved me the trouble. "Lunch is ready," he said.

After lunch Dad dragged Uncle Dave down to the Ford Motor Company to look at new cars.

Auntie Rose wanted to go downtown shopping. She always got wonderful bargains in Detroit, she said.

We watched them disappear behind the leafy trees on Newport Street, then Bart rubbed his hands together and said, "Okay, let's go to the show. I got American dough burning a hole in my pocket." He pulled out a wad of dollar bills.

Strolling along Jefferson Street, we bumped into Pam

and Kitty coming out of the Five and Dime. Shoot, I thought. I had a feeling I knew what was coming. Bart stopped and gave Pam the kind of goofy grin that boys give pretty girls. "How would you two like to come to the show with us, eh? I got lots of money," he bragged, flashing his dollar bills.

"I'd love to!" cried Pam. Slipping her arm through Bart's she did a little skip and they fell into step. The rest of us trailed along behind them.

When we got to the Cinderella Theatre we couldn't find seats together. So Pam sat with Bart, and Carrie and I sat behind them with Kitty. Jimmy had to sit in the front row by himself — his favourite place.

Right through the movie, Pam's and Bart's heads were stuck together like Siamese twins. We had to keep stretching our necks to see around them, and even then we could only see the sides of the movie screen.

* * *

That night Uncle Dave and Auntie Rose took us all out to dinner at the Black Steer restaurant. We were all allowed to order drinks. The men had beers and the women had Pink Ladies and all us kids had Shirley Temples with cherries at the bottom of the glass.

When we got back home in the Durante — Uncle Dave had resisted a new Ford — we watched Ed Sullivan together. Right in the middle of the Fabulous Fantino Family's balancing act, the phone rang. "Oh, shoot!" Mom said and went to the kitchen to answer it. She came back with a puzzled frown. "It's for you, Bart. It's a girl's voice."

"Uh-oh." Carrie and I read each other's minds again. Sure enough, it was Pamela Potter inviting our cousin to her house. But Uncle Dave said he couldn't go, so Bart sulked the rest of the evening and the next morning they went home.

Chapter 33

The Letter

After our Canadian visitors left, summer holidays got very boring. I almost wished it was time for school to start. Then one morning Mom picked up the mail that had just dropped through the letter slot and landed on the hall floor. Shuffling through them she muttered, "Bills, bills, bills." Then she held an envelope up to the light. "There's a letter here from Port Huron," she said curiously. "I wonder who it could be from?"

"Who's it for?" asked Robbie. He was at the kitchen table working on his Television Tips notebook.

"It's for you, Connie," Mom said, handing it to me.

I recognized the neat, round handwriting right away, so I ripped open the envelope. "It's from Wendy Johnson," I told Mom.

I had often thought of Wendy since she'd gone to live with her aunt. But I didn't have her address so it was as if she had disappeared without a trace. Like on Dragnet. That's what Sergeant Friday always says: The missing person disappeared without a trace.

166 River Road,
Port Huron, Michigan
Aug. 10, 1954

Dear Connie,

I'm sorry I didn't write sooner, but at first I was too sorrowful to put pen to paper. And I kept getting worse instead of better so my Aunt Sally took me to a doctor. Not a doctor doctor, a child psychiatrist. Her name is Dr. Edwina Waxman. She has short bleached-blonde hair and a kind smile and she is really nice. I talk to her twice a week and she helps me understand about, you know — what happened in my family. I'll tell you all about it when you get here. Oh, I haven't asked you yet, have I? Aunt Sally says you can come to stay with us for a week if your mother will let you travel alone on the bus. It's quite safe, she says, because you don't have to change buses. You just get on in Detroit and we'll meet you here at the bus station. You'll like my Aunt Sally and my Uncle Bernie, Connie. They are older than my own parents and their children are all grown up and married so I am an only child again. But I am not lonely like I was before because I am allowed to have friends now. I have made some nice friends here, but not as nice as you, Connie. You are special. Can you come? I have some amazing news to tell you. Too amazing to put in a letter. Please write back immediately.

Your loving friend,
Wendy Johnson.

P.S. Oh, I reminded my aunt that you are a twin and she says your sister can come too, if she likes. W.J.

I gave the letter to my mother. As she read it she looked skeptical. "On a bus? Alone? I don't know. We'll have to take it up with your father."

"If Carrie goes, I won't be alone. Where is she?"

"On the back porch drying her hair."

I went out and sat with her on the top step. Her hair was gleaming like butterscotch taffy in the sun. "Why aren't you using our hair dryer?" I asked.

"Because I love the way the sun bleaches my hair," she said, fluffing the soft feather cut with her fingers.

"Well, look there . . ." I pointed to her pudgy nose. "You've got four new freckles."

"Oh, freckles, speckles." Carrie wrinkled her nose. Then she noticed the letter in my hand. "Who's that from?" she asked.

"Read it," I said.

As she read her nose wrinkled some more. "Thanks, but no thanks. She doesn't even remember my name. Why should I go there?"

"Because I don't think Dad will let me go alone."

"Well, I'm not going." She jumped up and left me sitting there.

* * *

Dad surprised all of us by saying I could go on the bus alone, that it would be a good experience for me. And Carrie could stay home if she liked.

So Mom phoned Wendy's Aunt Sally and they had a nice chat. "She seems a lovely person." Mom said as she hung up the receiver. "I'm so glad for Wendy. And I'm sure you'll be fine with them, Connie."

That night I leaned over the rail of my bunk. "Carrie . . . " I said.

"What?"

"Are you going to see Pamela Potter while I'm gone?"

She flopped over on her back and looked up at me. Even in the moonlight I could see her extra freckles.

"I don't think so," she said. "She made me mad the way she flirted with Bart. Maybe I'll call for Kitty. She's dumb but she's a lot nicer than Pam."

I sighed with relief and snuggled down to sleep. I wasn't the least bit jealous of Kitty Foxcroft.

* * *

I sat beside a really cute boy on the bus. His name was Alvin Shoemaker and he was getting off at the stop before mine so I had company most of the way. We exchanged addresses and promised to write. And I did the strangest thing. As the bus swung into the Port Huron bus terminal, I realized I hadn't told him I had an identical twin. For a moment, I felt like a traitor to Carrie, even though I hadn't done it on purpose. Then I wondered.

I stepped off the bus and the driver got my suitcase.

"CONNIE!" Wendy screamed and came running toward me. I could hardly believe it was her, she had changed so much. Her thin sandy-coloured hair was thick and curly (probably a Toni, I thought) and her blueberry eyes looked bigger and brighter in her sun-tanned face. And she was taller than me now, when she used to be shorter.

I had forgotten how pretty her aunt was. She looked like Claudette Colbert's double, with her short brown hair and bangs that touched her eyebrows.

Aunt Sally — that's what she told me to call her —

drove a blue Ford Fairlaine. I'll tell Dad about it, I thought.

After a long drive we pulled into the circular gravel driveway of a beautiful white frame house. It had two big verandas, one upstairs and one down.

"That's my room up there." Wendy pointed to a glass door leading out onto an upstairs veranda. "We can sleep out there if we if we like."

"That sounds like fun," I said. You sure couldn't sleep outside on the veranda in Detroit, I thought.

Wendy grabbed my suitcase and ran with it into the house and up the central staircase. Her room was twice as big as Carrie's and mine, and all the furniture matched.

At the dinner table Wendy's Uncle Bernie, a jolly, paunchy man with a fringe of black hair around his pink shiny head, said to me, "So, I recall you have a twin at home. Do you still look alike?"

"Just a minute and I'll show you," I said, then I went to get my purse. Mom had bought me a little straw purse with daisies on it for the trip.

The snapshot of Carrie and me standing on our front steps in our Easter outfits surprised even me. Wendy's uncle passed his hand over his eyes as if to clear his vision. "You look like Tweedle-dum and Tweedle-dee," he laughed as he handed the picture to his wife.

She gave a little gasp. "Which one are you, Connie?" she asked.

I had to concentrate. Which side of the step had I been standing on? Then I remembered that the sleeve of my Easter coat had got caught on a thorn.

"That's me," I said, "standing beside Mom's rosebush."

Wendy looked at the picture and sighed. "Having a twin seems like having a lifelong best friend," she said.

"Yes." I nodded my head and put the picture back in my little straw purse. "But it's nice having other friends, too."

That night Wendy and I talked until two in the morning. Her bed was a big four-poster so there was lots of room for both of us. And her uncle never once hollered at us to settle down.

The first thing I asked her was what was the amazing news she couldn't put in her letter.

She took a deep breath and said, "I've seen my father!"

"Your father?" I had always thought Wendy's father was dead.

"Yes, my father." Her eyes were glittering like stars in the darkness. "He went to our house in Detroit and got a terrible shock when he found it was sold."

"But how did he ever find you here?" I was almost as thrilled as Wendy. Imagine how I would feel if I thought my dad was dead and then he turned up alive on our doorstep. I shivered with delight at the idea.

"Well, he got in touch with cousins I didn't even know I had and old friends I'd never met. And finally he found somebody who knew where I was. Then one night he telephoned. At first Aunt Sally and Uncle Bernie tried to keep him away from me. Then Aunt Sally talked to my psychiatrist, and she helped me decide if I wanted to see him or not. And I said I did and he came."

She stopped talking then, and stayed quiet for such a long time I thought she'd dropped off to sleep. Then I saw a shiny tear sliding down her cheek.

"Aren't you glad he found you?" I whispered.

"I am now," she said, wiping the tear away. "At first I wasn't sure because we were nearly strangers. But once I got to know him I really liked him. When we talked we really understood each other. My mother always said I took after him. I think that's the part of me she didn't like."

"That's amazing." A shiver crept down my spine. "And now that he's found you, does he want you back?"

"Oh, no. He knows I'm happy here with my aunt and uncle. He's a travelling salesman, you see, and he said that's no life for a girl. Dr. Waxman agreed with him but she said that was the turning point for me, finding my father. Have you noticed anything else different about me, Connie?"

"Yes!" I cried. "You don't stutter anymore."

* * *

Aunt Sally had planned a whole list of things for us to do: picnics and swimming and drive-in movies. And every day she took us to a different place, sightseeing. But what Wendy and I liked to do best was to sit outside on the upstairs veranda and talk and talk and talk.

I couldn't get over Wendy. She was like a new person. I had always liked her and considered her my special friend, but this new Wendy was so smart and interesting and self-confident that I hardly recognized her. She didn't seem like the same person as the nervous, stuttery little girl I used to know.

The day before I was to leave for home Aunt Sally said to me, "How would you like to come to Pebble Beach with us for a week, Connie? Bernie and I have rented a cabin there and we'd love to have you."

150

"Oh, yes, Connie." Wendy's blue eyes sparkled with excitement. "Please say you'll come."

"Sure!" I cried. "But my mother is expecting me."

"Oh, don't worry,' said Aunt Sally, "I'll call your mother tonight when the rates are lower, and make sure it's all right." She gave us both a big squeeze. "Now you two go and sort out your dirty laundry. I'd like to do a load or two before we start packing."

Wendy and I ran right upstairs. In the middle of my sorting, I had to go to the bathroom. As I was washing my hands I glanced in the mirror above the sink — and there was Carrie staring out at me.

"Go away!" I said, and hurried back to Wendy's bedroom. But Carrie and I had never been separated this long before, and my conscience was pricking me like a needle.

I stopped with my bathing suit in my hands. "I can't go," I said to Wendy.

"Why not?" Wendy gave me a puzzled frown. "Are you homesick?"

"No. But I feel my twin sister missing me."

Wendy sighed wistfully. "I think I understand," she said. "We'd better go tell Aunt Sally."

Wendy tried not to mind, but I could tell she was disappointed. And when I boarded the Detroit-bound bus and waved goodbye for the second time to my best friend, I wasn't happy, either.

Chapter 34

Betrayal

I thought Carrie would be there to meet me at the bus depot but Mom was alone on the platform. I caught sight of her through the window while I waited my turn to get off.

She had on a new summer dress and Aunt Sylvia must have done her hair because the dark curls framed her face like a picture. When she caught sight of me she flashed me a smile and I noticed how pretty she was. For the hundred-millionth time I wished us twins had taken after our mom instead of our dad.

"Where's Carrie?" was the first thing I asked as I hopped off the bus.

"She's over at Pamela Potter's," Mom said, picking up my suitcase.

"Pamela Potter's!" I shouted. I was mad. "What happened to Kitty Foxcroft?"

"Well, Kitty went camping with her family and Carrie got lonely. Did you have a good time with Wendy?"

"Yes. A super-duper time. In fact, I could have stayed

longer, but I thought Carrie would want me back home." I was still mad.

Mom stroked my hair. "Well, I'm glad to see you," she said, smiling. "Were Wendy's aunt and uncle nice?"

"Really nice. They didn't care how long we stayed awake talking. And do you know what? Wendy met her father!"

"Her father? I thought Mr. Johnson was dead."

"So did I."

We got on the Jefferson Avenue bus and were lucky enough to find a seat together, so I could tell Mom all about Wendy's new life on the way home. When we walked in our front door I had the strangest feeling everything was smaller than when I left. Even the French doors seemed to have shrunk. Then the telephone rang in the kitchen.

I ran and grabbed it up and cried, "Hi Carrie! I'm home!"

There was a moment's silence. Then a woman's voice said, "May I speak to Mrs. Taylor, please?"

I handed Mom the phone and tried to eavesdrop.

As she listened Mom's eyebrows knitted together. "Well, I guess it will be all right," she said. "But she should come home first thing in the morning. Thank you. Goodbye." She hung up the phone and began unpacking my suitcase on the kitchen table. "My goodness, all your clothes are fresh and clean," she exclaimed, sniffing my nightgown.

"What do you mean, first thing in the morning? Isn't Carrie coming home tonight?" I asked suspiciously.

"That was Pamela's mother. Mr. Potter wants to take the girls to the outdoor symphony concert over on Belle

Isle tonight." She refolded my nightgown and put it on top of the pile. "They'll be late getting home so Carrie is going to stay overnight."

"My news will be stale as mouldy bread by then!" I pouted.

"Well, you can always tell your father and brothers."

Disappointed, I picked up my pile of clean clothes and went upstairs to put them away in my side of the dresser.

That night I went to bed early. I was very tired — I had been up late every night for the past week. But for some reason I couldn't go to sleep.

Mom and Dad peeked in on their way to bed and were surprised that I was still awake. "Are you okay?" Mom asked.

"Sure, but I can't get to sleep."

"You're just excited to be home," Dad said. "I'll get you an aspirin to help settle you down."

He brought me two pink children's aspirins and a glass of warm water from the tap.

"Thanks, Daddy," I said. I hadn't called him Daddy in a month of Sundays.

"Want the door left open a crack?" he asked. He usually made us shut it.

"Sure," I said. The cuckoo clock in the kitchen cuckooed eleven times.

"Tomorrow that thing goes in the garbage," I heard Dad say as they walked to their room.

"If it goes, the green panther goes with it," countered Mom.

"You win," Dad chuckled.

Hours went by and the aspirins didn't seem to be

154

working. I wished I had gone to Pebble Beach with Wendy after all. I had come home for Carrie's sake, and she was so busy individuating with Pamela Potter that she didn't even notice.

I was just thinking about writing it all down in my diary when a flash of pain in my right leg made me sit bolt upright.

"Mom!" I called, close to tears. Then the phone rang. Mom and Dad must have been sound asleep because it was Robbie who switched on the hall light and padded down the stairs to answer it. Then he yelled up in a shrill voice, "MOM! DAD!"

Their door flew open and they rushed to the top of the stairs. I hobbled after them, pain shooting through my leg.

"What is it?" cried Mom.

"Who in blazes would be calling at this hour?" grumbled Dad.

Robbie's tanned face was the colour of sand. "It's the hospital," he whispered hoarsely.

"Hospital? What hospital?" Dad looked confused, but Mom knew instinctively. "It's Carrie! Something's happened to my Carrie!" She flew down the stairs to the phone.

* * *

No-one had to tell me that Carrie had been hurt, and that the injury was to her left leg. The pain in my right one was excruciating. I limped into the kitchen and collapsed on a chair, drawing my leg up to my chest. It felt as if my leg had been sliced open with a knife. I even looked to see if it was bleeding. It wasn't, but I could feel every throb of blood going through it.

Mom and Dad hurried back upstairs to get dressed. On the way out the door Mom cried, "We'll call from the hospital."

"But— but— I have to go, too!" I jumped up, and moaned in pain. Mom was too upset to notice.

"You stay here with Robbie," Dad said. "We'll let you know."

Before I could say another word they were gone.

Jimmy had slept right through it all, so Robbie and I were alone in the kitchen. He got two tumblers down from the cupboard and a quart of milk from the Frigidaire. I just sat there rubbing my leg.

"What's wrong with your leg?" he asked.

"There's a terrible pain in it," I said, and to my surprise I burst out crying.

"Is it that bad?"

"Yes!"

Robbie ran upstairs and came back with the aspirin bottle. Not baby aspirins this time, real ones.

"Here," he said, dumping two tablets on the table, "take these with your milk."

I did but they didn't help much. I was worried sick about Carrie.

Chapter 35

The Perfect Match

I sat in the kitchen nursing my leg for what seemed like hours, waiting for the phone to ring. When it did I nearly jumped out of my skin.

"Connie . . ." It was Mom. "Carrie is badly hurt . . ." She started to cry and I thought my heart would explode. Then Dad came on the line. "Let me speak to Robbie," he said.

My hand was shaking so much I dropped the receiver.

Robbie grabbed it up and listened. "Yes, Dad. Okay, Dad. I'll take care of things here. Tell Carrie— " He stopped to listen. "Well, when she wakes up tell her we're all pulling for her."

When she wakes up! Pulling for her! Just then Jimmy came into the kitchen yawning and rubbing his eyes. "What's going on? Where is everybody? Who are we pulling for?"

"Carrie's in the hospital. She got hurt in a car accident. Dad says she's still asleep," was Robbie's nervous answer.

The word "asleep" made me suspicious. "Do you mean asleep or unconscious?" I asked fearfully.

"I'm not sure. Dad says he'll call back soon. I'll turn the ringer up so we'll be sure to hear it." He slid the switch on the side of the phone from low to high. "C'mon, we may as well watch T.V."

I looked at the cuckoo clock. Just then the little wooden bird popped out and cuckooed three times.

"It's three o'clock in the morning," I said. "There won't be anything on."

"Okay, so let's check the test pattern to see how clear it is," he said.

So we followed Robbie to the living room and Jimmy jumped into the La-Z-Boy. "Get out of there!" Robbie dumped him on the floor. "Connie, you sit here and put your leg up."

I lay back and closed my eyes. The pain was pulsing through my calf like electric shocks. Regretful thoughts tumbled through my mind. If only Carrie had kept her promise not to have anything to do with Pam. If only she had come to Port Huron with me. If only I had been nicer to her. If only I wasn't so selfish. If only I had stayed home. If . . . if . . . if . . .

I needed to go to the bathroom so I crawled up the stairs on my hands and knees.

I was washing my hands, resting my right foot on my left to ease the pain, when I happened to glance in the medicine cabinet mirror. And there she was, my mirror image, staring out at me with those gold-speckled green eyes. My hand shook as I lifted my hair above my bent right ear. In the mirror it was Carrie's bent left ear. I blinked and she blinked. I opened my mouth to scream and so did she. Then I remembered Aunt Sylvia telling me about four-year-old Carrie gazing at herself in the hand mirror and saying, "I don't know who I are."

I whispered to the mirror. "I don't know who I are, either."

Suddenly I had a terrible, horrifying thought. What if my twin sister died? For the rest of my life, every time I looked in the mirror I would see her instead of me.

I sat down on the toilet seat, trembling from head to toe. Wild, crazy notions went flashing through my mind. "If a twin is all I am," I whispered, "what will I be without her?"

The phone gave a piercing ring, shattering my thoughts.

Robbie had the receiver pressed to his ear as I limped into the kitchen. His face fell and he closed his eyes as he listened. Then he said, "Yes, Dad. I'll tell her." He hung up the phone.

"Is Carrie dead?" Jimmy put our worst fear into words.

"No!" Robbie took him by the shoulders and shook him. Then he turned to me. "Dad's on his way home to get you, Connie."

"To get me? What for?"

"I don't know. He just said for you to be dressed and ready. Is your leg all right?"

"Yes," I lied. Then I staggered back upstairs to get dressed.

* * *

Boris Karloff came roaring up the street and screeched to a stop in front of the house.

"Hurry, Connie!" Dad yelled.

159

"What's happening, Dad?" Robbie and Jimmy ran to the curb.

"There's no time. I'll explain later."

Dad drove at top speed, staring straight ahead. "What happened, Dad?" I asked in a shaky whisper.

He kept his eyes on the road. "On the way home from Belle Isle Mr. Potter's car was hit by a drunk driver running a red light." I had to strain to hear because he was talking through clenched teeth. "The car hit the side where Carrie was sitting."

My heart began to pound. "Is she hurt bad?"

"Pretty bad."

"Is Pam hurt, too?"

"No. She was just shaken up. The doctor gave her a sedative and Mr. Potter took her home."

We were nearly there when we heard a siren screaming.

"Oh, Lord!" Dad cried, pulling over to the shoulder of the road. The police car parked behind us and Dad rolled down the window. Before the policeman could say a word Dad said, "I have to get to the hospital, Officer. My daughter may be dying."

Dying! My heart lurched in my chest.

The policeman looked at me.

"Not this one," Dad explained, "the other one."

The fear on our faces must have convinced him because he cried, "Follow me!" Then, with lights flashing and siren wailing he escorted us to the Emergency doors in five minutes flat.

Mom and a doctor with a grey beard in a white coat and a stethoscope around his neck came rushing toward us. Mom held out her arms and I ran into them. Then they took me to a room marked VISITORS and sat me down on a chair.

"Connie . . ." The doctor crouched down in front of me and took both my hands. Somebody must have told him my name. "Your sister severed an artery in her leg and she's lost a lot of blood."

"Her left leg?" I asked.

"Yes. How did you know?"

"Because my right leg is killing me."

"Oh, Connie!" Mom understood immediately. "They often feel each other's pain," she explained.

The doctor wagged his head, perplexed. "Well, your sister has a very rare blood type that the hospital doesn't have in the blood bank. And neither of your parents has it either. But when they told me Carrie had an identical twin, then I knew we had a match."

"Can I give it to her and save her life?" I cried.

"Yes. Are you ready?"

He didn't have to ask me twice.

He took me into a little cubicle and helped me up onto a stretcher. Then he swabbed my left arm with iodine and stuck a big needle in, draining off a whole bag of blood.

When he had enough I said, "Can I come and watch you pour it in?"

"No." He almost chuckled. "You stay right there. I'll send your parents in to sit with you."

Mom and Dad drew up chairs on either side of the stretcher and held my hands. We didn't talk, we just waited.

Suddenly I felt a sharp pain in my right arm and I went all woozy. Then I had the strangest feeling that

Carrie was inside of me, or I was inside of her, I didn't know which. I must have fallen asleep because I opened my eyes and the doctor was smiling down at me, stroking his beard. "She's awake!" he said.

"Who?" I asked groggily.

"Your sister. And her cheeks are getting pinker by the minute, thanks to your special gift, Connie."

I blinked. I hadn't even remembered to bring Carrie a present from Port Huron. "What gift?"

"Your rare and wonderful blood." He helped me sit up. "She's asking for you."

"I'll carry her," Dad said. And he picked me up in his arms like a baby.

"Mom," I said, over his shoulder. "The pain's all gone from my leg now."

She smiled with tears in her eyes and patted my hand that was wrapped around Dad's neck.

We were taken into the recovery room where a long white drape, like a shower curtain, encircled a bed. The doctor flung it open.

And there she was, my mirror image, smiling weakly, but alive, her cheeks as pink as cotton candy. Dad set me down on the bed beside her and she took my hand.

"Connie," she said in a shaky whisper. "The doctor says you saved my life."

"Well, sure," My voice was shaky, too. "What's a twin for?"

"Oh, Connie, I'm sorry about always wanting to individuate. I won't do it anymore," she promised.

I remembered her face in the bathroom mirror. And I heard the words: I don't know who I are.

"Maybe it's a good idea that we both individuate sometimes," I said.

162

She stared at me, then smiled, and I knew she understood. "Okay!" she agreed.

I thought of something else. "You'll have a scar on your left leg now. We won't be identical anymore anyway."

"Well, whenever we want to be identical we can wear twin stockings," Carrie said.

We all laughed and then the doctor said, "My patient needs to rest now."

So I kissed my sister good night, and we went home.

BERNICE THURMAN HUNTER was a storyteller from an early age, but it was not until her children were grown that she began to get her work published. Now she is one of Canada's favourite writers of historical fiction, with a dozen books to her credit, including the *Booky* and *Margaret* trilogies, *Lamplighter* and *Janey's Choice*.

Bernice has also earned many awards: *Amy's Promise* won the 1997 Red Cedar Award, and in 1989 Bernice was honoured with the Vicky Metcalf Award for her contribution to Canadian children's literature.